Elephant in the Room

Elephant in the Room

A novel
by
Kristen Harper

Dove
Publishers

Encouraging words for Elephant in the Room

"This fantastic book moves beyond health guidelines and tips on will-power to compassionately address the forgotten sin of gluttony. With humility and kindness, it outlines the process of recognizing the sin of gluttony in our lives, confessing it Biblically, and relying on the power of Christ to overcome. I don't lightly recommend a Christian novel on sin issues, but this is so much more. It confronts many of our cultural preconceptions that blind us to gluttony. My favorite character is Nick Saint, a Christian and professional Santa Claus, who struggles with the perception that he should look "jiggly!" Overall: a great book that I couldn't finish reading without prayer and repentance." – *Corrie Garrett, author of the Alien Cadet trilogy.*

"In Elephant in the Room, Harper accurately identifies obesity as not just a physical problem, but one that is rooted in the heart. The subject of gluttony is handled with sensitivity and practical Biblical application, and readers will find it as instructive as it is encouraging. It is refreshing to see such an important topic brought to the forefront." - *Liana Hofer, Marketing Coordinator, Children's Hunger Fund.*

"This is an important topic for the local church as it exposes one of the respectable sins that believers can be prone to coddle. The setting and conflicts have a "real world" tone to them. I think it is important to delve into these areas and understand the role of the Holy Spirit in all such matters of Christian testimony and sanctification. The encouragement toward Biblical counseling is great and well done. This will be a hard message for most people to apply for the reasons the book illustrates – people have their own excuses and habits." – *Bryan McKinney, Director, International Outreach, Joni and Friends International Disability Center.*

For more comments, visit the author's website at:
KristenHarperBooks.WordPress.com

Elephant in the Room
Published by Dove Christian Publishers
P.O. Box 611
Bladensburg, MD 20710-0611
www.dovechristianpublishers.com

Copyright © 2017 by Kristen Harper

Author photo by Rachel Harper

Library of Congress Control Number: 2017940957

ISBN: 978-0-9975898-7-0

Printed in the United States of America

This book is dedicated to Angela de Moura, a dear friend who invited me to participate in two amazing Bible-focused ministries, the National Bible Bee and the food Bible study called The Lord's Table.

Chapter 1

Candlelight flickered warmly. The long red tapers stood erect in their brass holders like lighthouses signaling their locations, beacons calling some to draw near while warning others to avoid a destructive crash.

The mirror behind the sideboard reflected the candles' flames, casting a pleasant and festive glow on the dining room. Spread across the table were many casserole dishes, deep bowls with spoon handles protruding over the edge, and serving platters stacked precariously on racks. Except for a few cold dishes, everything steamed with fragrant, savory aromas of the season. There was no room for decorative ornaments or even a fall centerpiece; the woven tablecloth in autumn hues was barely visible under the serving dishes.

The mashed potatoes were flecked with green scallions while the fragrance revealed generous doses of butter and garlic. Brown-speckled wild rice competed with golden-yellow cornbread stuffing piled too high in matching bowls. Rosemary. Oregano. Sage. Savory scents abounded. Displayed on a long platter, a line of small acorn squash had been hollowed out, the contents blended with seasonings and sweetness before being whipped up and dolloped decoratively back into their shells. They looked good enough to eat!

In the basket, the forest green napkin barely wrapping around the fresh hot bread could not restrain the comforting odor of yeast from mingling with the other familiar scents. Golden cornbread muffins were speckled with yellow corn kernels and green chilies while the dark pumpkin bread slices revealed their treasure of walnuts and raisins. The butter had been molded into pretty shapes. It would almost be a shame to cut into them, but the spread was needed for the bread and freshly steamed corn.

Which would be the favorite this year, the traditional dark cranberry sauce or the light cranberry relish which was chopped fine with oranges? A beautiful layered Jello was cubed so that each piece revealed a creamy-white base with thin lines of fall colors: red, orange, yellow and green. The scent of cinnamon wafted from the baked apples with just a hint of cloves.

There was, of course, a large, creamy green bean casserole, its border generously sprinkled with fried onions, a classic and family favorite. Other greens were displayed in their more natural state, such as the tossed fresh spinach salad and lightly steamed asparagus, the hollandaise sauce served from a small gravy boat nearby. More elaborate vegetable dishes were created by frying the okra or glazing the carrots with honey and brown sugar.

While the table was overflowing with food, the sideboard remained, temporarily, less crowded. Several pies, a few cakes and a variety of cookies and candy left a little space to set out the cold accouterments later: ice cream in several flavors, including vanilla, and pure white mountains of homemade whipped cream.

At just the right time, a gigantic ceramic platter was brought to the place of honor amid this bountiful spread. The thirty-pound Thanksgiving turkey glowed as the candlelight shone on its glossy brown skin braised with herbs and spices. The steam wafted into Eric Harvey's face as he hefted the platter into place. He looked around the room, pleased.

"Wow! What a feast!" he exclaimed to his wife Jennifer and her mother Beverly as they glided out of the kitchen with even more food to add to the table. "It looks like we have enough food for thirty people!"

Beverly and Jennifer giggled delightedly at the compliment. "Well, we do like to go all out for Thanksgiving," exuded Beverly, "but it's just our little family this year." Her son Darren's family couldn't come to town over the short Thanksgiving break. Eric's parents were spending this holiday with his sister's family in California.

The other family members soon gathered around the dining table. Beverly's husband Leonard Douglas hauled himself out of the recliner to stand by Beverly who, although she had been slaving away in the kitchen most of the day, had taken a few moments to return her frosted crop of hair into place and add bright lipstick to match the flush in her cheeks. Leonard patted her on the back and smiled lovingly at her before he leaned on a nearby chair. He looked across the bountiful table at his daughter Jennifer, whose darker coloring matched his. Her smile, resembling her mother's, beamed with delight while she hosted this smaller family gathering this year in her suburban Albany, Georgia home. Eric called their children to join them. Hannah, who had been trying to convince her grandpa Leonard to take her out to practice driving over the weekend, scrambled up from the floor, unfolding the long limbs of a growing teenager to spring up as tall as her mom. Twelve-year-old Samuel had been sitting on the sofa showing his big brother Chris and Chris's wife Ashley his latest book about African animals. The children came over to complete the circle around the table. Everyone commented about the sights and smells of the delicious food spread out before them.

Even though it was his house and he was the pastor of the local church, Eric honored his father-in-law by asking him to say the blessing before the meal. As everyone held hands and bowed their heads, Leonard intoned in his strong voice.

"Dear Lord, we thank You for this bountiful food. Your blessings come through the hard work of our dear ladies who planned and cooked this meal that we are delighted to share with our family. Lord, we thank You for Your numerous blessings from this past year, and we look to You to strengthen us and refine us through the coming year with all of its trials, temptations, and blessings. Great is our God and greatly to be praised. Amen." The others echoed the amen.

"Let's spend a few minutes going around the table for everyone to thank God for something He has done for us this past year." Leonard paused to give everyone a moment to think about what they wanted to say. Then he started the list. "I'm thankful for 49 years of marriage to this wonderful gal!"

"Oh Leonard," gushed Beverly like a new bride. "You say the sweetest things to me! You know how thankful I am for you, and for renewed strength and health for you after a few health challenges this year. I'm especially thankful to God for my precious family!" she announced enthusiastically.

"Now, Grandma, you say that every year," teased Hannah.

"Well, when it stops being true, then I'll stop saying it," replied Beverly, laughing with her granddaughter.

"I'm thankful for growing up and getting more opportunities for adventures, like driving," said Hannah, looking hopefully at her parents and grandpa.

"With those opportunities for adventure also comes responsibility," reminded her father, "but we're thankful to the Lord to be around to watch you growing into a lovely young lady."

Hannah blushed sweetly.

Eric continued. "It has been a great joy for me to watch many of the youth in our church growing up over the past twenty years in this congregation. We've had weddings of former nursery students, and we've welcomed the next generation of little ones into the fold when their parents stay connected to God and church attendance. Thank You, God, for blessing our ministry to Your people."

"Yes, Lord," chimed in Jennifer after her husband's praise. "And I'm thankful for the new people we have come to know in the past year. New friends!" She thought about several families who had joined the church as well as a few single older people looking for Christian fellowship to enjoy on their walk of life.

"My turn," broke in Samuel enthusiastically. "I'm thankful that God made all the different animals! Does anyone know what my favorite animal is?"

"Last year it was the cheetah, son, last month it was an ocelot, and just last week you were raving about a sloth," chuckled Eric. "So, what exotic animal is your favorite now?"

"An elephant," Samuel stated matter-of-factly.

"An old classic and all-time favorite, to be sure," said his grand-father.

"Excuse me, Grandpa," interrupted Chris. "It will be two years in December that Ashley and I have been married. We're hoping to catch up to you and grandma, so watch yourselves. I'm thankful for our new house and how my wife has decorated it to make it such a nice place to come home to after a hard day at work."

"Thanksgiving at your house next year?" teased Eric. Jennifer elbowed him with a knowing look.

"Oh...I don't know about that," stammered Ashley, turning red. "I don't think I could make a meal like this yet."

"He's just teasing you, honey," comforted Jennifer. "We don't expect you to host until you're ready, but we sure appreciate the dishes you brought and your help in the kitchen today," she said encouragingly. "So, what are you thankful for, Ashley?"

"I'm thankful for your kindness to me, welcoming me into your family over the past few years. First, you Jennifer, mentoring and discipling me. I don't think you thought of me as your future daughter-in-law back in those early years of counseling. But now I have Chris, a lovely home of my own and a loving extended family with all the trimming like this meal here! It means a lot to me, coming from a broken home with hardly any traditions or celebrations," Ashley said humbly.

"Well, it's not our tradition to eat cold food on Thanksgiving, so let's wrap this up by saying thanks to God for these blessings and by loading up our plates!" Grandpa Leonard declared.

All of them piled their plates high with their favorite holiday foods. With so much food on display in the dining room, a separate table was set and decorated in the living room for the family to gather around. Lively chat around the table continued about things each person was thankful for over the past year. Grandpa's health was reviewed, the children's achievements were discussed, and church events were remembered fondly.

In their mid-seventies, Leonard and Beverly were both extremely overweight. While Beverly still maintained an active life serving her family and friends in the community, Leonard had become more sedentary. Yet when Beverly called him for help, he still came running to try to do the same things he used to be able to handle as a young Marine. On several occasions, he had strained his back, and his legs, which were already enduring the extra burden of weight, had started failing under him, causing him to stumble and fall. These personal accidents had brought him into the hospital where they had begun to monitor his cholesterol, blood pressure and blood sugar levels. Beverly tried to soothe Leonard in her usual fashion, baking delicious treats in her pristine white kitchen of the home they had shared most of their married life together.

Eric married their elder daughter Jennifer about twenty-five years ago, shortly after he had finished Bible Seminary. He served as an Associate Pastor of Grace Community Church in Albany, Georgia, for a few years before he was called to take over when the older pastor retired. Eric's square shoulders caused his preaching suits to hang handsomely when he was standing before his congregation even when his curly hair was a bit disheveled. That, along with a friendly smile, gave him a boyish charm even at his age, as he was now closer to fifty than forty. Around home and on weekdays, he preferred polo shirts, jeans, and sturdy boots. His sons Chris and Samuel had inherited his mop of disheveled locks and boyish grin. Hannah was disappointed with her straight brown hair from her mother, but she tried not to mope about it, hoping it would begin to thicken to grow long and strong like her mother's had. Until then, she frequently pulled it back in a ponytail. Thankfully, her brother Samuel was forbidden from tugging on it, but since she didn't see Chris as often anymore, he still had big-brother-teasing-ponytail-pulling privileges.

After a short time, several people rose from their chairs to head back to the dining room for seconds. "Does it count as 'seconds' if we just get things that we didn't get to try on our first plate?" Eric tried to ask reasonably. There were still many dishes that were, in fact, untouched from the first go-round but now would be attacked with serving spoons. Favorites began to dwindle. Back at the family table, more conversations continued as the plates were cleaned again, a little slower than the first time but just as thoroughly. Ashley enjoyed talking to Jennifer and Beverly about some of the decorating ideas for her new house. Hannah listened in and offered to go shopping with her anytime. Since Ashley had been around the Harvey house for years, Hannah grew up loving and respecting Ashley as a cool older sister and had been only too delighted to serve as a junior bridesmaid when Ashley married her big brother. The men moved to settle into the recliners and sofas as they were looking forward to the football games coming up in the afternoon.

"So, Dad, do those athletes have a Thanksgiving meal at home or together with their team before the game?" Samuel asked in his usual curious, but slightly concerned way.

"They're in training, son, so I don't think they would have this kind of meal before a big game," Eric gestured back to their family's big spread as he explained what he thought was probably true. "Not only do they miss out on the traditional food but they miss out on the family gathering on this day."

"I hope they have a big family celebration on another day, maybe even tomorrow after the games," suggested Samuel. "But they can't have our leftovers. We have plans for those!"

Later, Eric and his father-in-law Leonard stretched out in the comfortable overstuffed recliners in the den. On the side table, they each had a plate scattered with an assortment of the desserts. They worked on these treats over the next few hours of the games. Eric almost upset his plate once when the game action got exciting. They both snoozed in their comfortable chairs, but they were often interrupted by different family members. Chris kept them updated on the games if their eyes were closed for too long. Samuel sat playing with his African animal figurines, squaring the elephant to face off with the rhinoceros and wildebeest, then racing the cheetah against the ostrich and giraffe. Hannah was checking to see if her grandpa would take her out in the car, hoping he could be pried away at halftime. The ladies offered more goodies for the first half of each game and offered to remove their plates many times during the second half of those games, but they were reluctant to give them up until everything had been sampled. Occasional bursts of laughter could be heard coming from the kitchen as the young ladies enjoyed special bonding time with Jennifer and Beverly over a sink full of dishes. It was a comfortable and sweet time with family.

Chapter 2

"Good night, Grandpa! Good night, Grandma! Thank you for the delicious pies," Samuel called out into the dark night as Leonard and Beverly were getting into their car. "And thanks for leaving the leftovers! I'll share if you come back over tomorrow."

Leonard gently pulled away from the curb. The headlights of their Toyota shined brightly through the dark neighborhood streets, empty now after 10:00 p.m. Leonard turned right onto the major street with several unoccupied lanes and headed for their home just a few miles away. They enjoyed the tree-lined avenue, noticing a few houses and apartment buildings with Christmas decorations already up. Beverly remembered that tomorrow she would start on her own Christmas decorating. It was a quiet drive after the hubbub of the family Thanksgiving meal.

"What a delightful evening with our family," sighed Beverly. "Those kids are getting bigger every time I see them."

"You see them every week, dear," teased Leonard, as he glanced in the rearview mirror to see a sleek car racing up behind him at high speed. After several more glances in the mirror, Leonard became concerned. "What's this guy doing?" exclaimed Leonard.

What happened next seemed like a slow nightmare. The car that Leonard had seen approaching slammed into the rear of their Toyota, catapulting them at an awkward angle toward the parked cars on the right side of the avenue. The sound of their screeching tires soon gave way to the stench of burning rubber. Leonard heard Beverly scream as he tried to control their car to no avail. The maniac driver's Cadillac high-performance sedan crushed Leonard's Toyota Camry like an accordion into a white, full-size Chevy truck parked at the curb before it spun out of control into a lamppost on the other side of the street. The grating noise of clashing metal rang out through the peaceful night. The air bags exploded for protection. Then all was silent.

After what seemed like hours in the cold, dark silence of the night, Leonard realized that he could feel metal pressed sharply against his body in several places. He tried to turn his head to check on Beverly, but pain shot through his neck. He called out to his beloved wife, "Beverly, Beverly! Are you all right?" but there was no response. While it felt like a lifetime, people soon came out of the surrounding houses and apartments. Cell phones lit up as some called the sheriff and the fire department for emergency services. The owner of the parked truck moaned loudly and ran his hands through his bed-head mop of hair while he gazed at his damaged vehicle. Other men and women rushed toward the accident looking for victims to help.

"Sir, are you awake? Can you tell me how you are?" one neighbor questioned Leonard assertively but with genuine concern as he peered through the shattered window, shining his cell phone light to look in.

"Yes, I think I lost consciousness for a moment, but I'm awake now. I can't move; I'm pinned in. But I can't see what's happened to my wife. I can't turn to look at her in the passenger seat. Please go check on her," Leonard pleaded.

Other neighbors circled around their car. One man, with his hand wrapped in a towel, wiped away the broken window glass to check on Beverly. "Ma'am, the rescue team is on their way. We're right here around you," he said, even though he could tell that Beverly was not conscious. Her eyes were closed, and her head drooped to one side. There was blood trickling from a gash on Beverly's head, but the airbags had done their job of protecting them from greater injury.

Thankfully, Leonard began to hear sirens getting closer. Before long, a paramedic in full emergency garb strode up to Leonard's window as he assessed the situation.

"Sir, we're here to help you. Can you tell me your name? Can you tell me how you feel?" the paramedic questioned.

"My name is Leonard Douglas. My wife Beverly and I were driving home from our Thanksgiving meal with our family. I'm stuck and can't turn my head to check on my wife." Leonard tried to answer clearly, but he was growing more concerned for Beverly.

"Thank you, Leonard. Can you tell me how you feel? Do you have pain or even loss of feeling anywhere?" again the paramedic questioned.

"I feel metal squeezing my legs and body. I feel sharp pains on the skin of my face and arms. Is my wife OK? We need to help her." Leonard pleaded again for his wife.

A fireman stepped over to explain. "Paramedics are already assisting her, sir. We need to assess the situation. You appear to be trapped. There is no immediate risk of fire, but we're going to take some precautions and cover your car with foam. That will give us time to get you released safely from the vehicle in order to take you to the emergency room for medical care." Next, the paramedic covered Leonard with a light blanket and moved away before a hiss signaled the spraying of the flame-retardant foam.

Leonard tried to wait patiently for further help but could feel his anxiety building as his heartbeat became louder in his ears. He listened as the fire officials coordinated with the police and paramedics to make plans for their rescue.

"The male driver is conscious, slight lacerations on his face and arms, but wedged into the seat between the steering wheel, airbags, and the crumpled frame. He has complained of pain and restriction in his neck. The female passenger is unconscious, possible concussion with trauma to her forehead, with multiple skin lacerations, and wedged in as well. We were unable to assess for breaks, so we'll have to treat her with care and possible neck injuries. Let's remove the doors first, then cut the frame away. These people are so fat that we can't pull them out easily."

Shame flooded Leonard's emotions. *Trapped. Wedged in. Too fat to be rescued.* He was thankful Beverly didn't hear that. He hoped she was unconscious at least for that. But then she moaned.

The next few minutes were spent carefully deconstructing their crumpled vehicle with the Jaws of Life to make a safe means to remove their traumatized bodies. Leonard was aware of the crushed tailgate in front of them, recognizing it as one from a new truck that had been safely parked on the avenue. He hoped that it had been empty. He wondered about the driver of the sporty luxury sedan that ran into them. A police officer was now on the scene and came over to question Leonard some more. Leonard was still stuck, but he was relieved to see the paramedics working to get Beverly out first.

"Mr. Douglas. I'm Officer Stanley. I go to church with you." Leonard recognized the young man. "Sir, if you're up to it, I'd like to ask you some more questions about this incident. Sometimes our memory is pretty clear right after the event. Can you tell me what you remember?" asked the officer as he pulled out his notebook and pen.

Leonard tried to explain, "My wife and I were driving home after our family celebration..."

The officer interrupted him. "Sir, did you drink any alcohol at the celebration? Anything at all?"

"No, sir!" Leonard responded with a sharp tone, then calmed down. "I'm not a drinking man. Our family does not serve alcohol at family events."

"Thank you for the information, sir. I had to ask."

Leonard took a few more minutes to describe for the officer how he had noticed the speeding car in the rear-view mirror as it raced towards them only seconds before impact. It happened so suddenly that there weren't many more details. He had seen no one else on the road. He gave Officer Stanley the home phone number for Eric and Jennifer, and he promised to contact them as soon as possible. Then, a whole squad of paramedics came to pull Leonard out of the vehicle. After covering Leonard's body with protective gear, the power saw rang out in the quiet night. Men carefully removed the metal framing pieces that had held him in. Leonard's neck was braced before they hefted him out and slid him onto the waiting gurney. Before he moved into the ambulance, he looked around for his wife.

"Where's my wife?" he shouted.

A nearby medic explained that she had been removed before him and was already on her way to the same hospital where he was going. But there was still another emergency vehicle on the scene. The back doors were open, waiting to receive the driver of the other car. Before Leonard left the scene, he saw a gurney sliding into the coroner's van, but the whole body, including the face, was covered. The driver was dead.

Chapter 3

Beverly woke the next morning in a sterile but warm hospital room. She noticed the familiar isopropyl alcohol smell after she discerned the beeps and hums of medical equipment surrounding her bed. Her head ached as she slowly opened her eyes. Even though the lights were probably dimmed, Beverly could see stars around the bulbs. To avoid nausea, she closed her eyes again but not before seeing her daughter leaning over and smiling at her.

"Good morning, Mom," soothed Jennifer. "It's good to see your beautiful blue eyes. Go ahead and rest. Squeeze my hand if you need something. Do you want water?"

After Beverly had squeezed her hand, Jennifer lifted the straw up to her mother's lips. Rather than lifting her head, she turned slightly to put her lips around the straw Jennifer held steadily for her. Beverly winced from the head rush of trying to move.

"Sorry, that seemed to strain you. Lay back, Mom. Do you have pain? Do you want me to get the nurse to help you manage the pain?"

Beverly squeezed her hand. Jennifer let go of her hand and stepped into the hallway to summon the nurse. In a few minutes, a cheerful older nurse came into the room with a tray of assorted medications and a comforting presence.

"Good morning, Mrs. Douglas. I am Nancy, the day nurse. The night crew took good care of you when you came in, but they went home a few hours ago. I'm happy to see that you are waking up, but

I'm sure you are still in a lot of pain. The doctor left instructions about some options, so let me make an assessment so that I can help you out. You have a lot of minor injuries, and combined, they can add up to a lot of pain," explained the efficient nurse.

After Nurse Nancy got Beverly comfortably situated, Jennifer began asking her mother questions about the accident. She didn't know if her mom would remember or even understand what had happened in the night. What a way to end such a lovely evening!

"I don't know what hit us!" exclaimed Beverly with a weary voice. "One minute we were enjoying the peaceful drive home, then your dad cried out about a car coming fast behind us right before we were knocked out." Beverly did not remember very many details, but she admitted to Jennifer that she had overheard the paramedic's comment about how fat she was. Tears welled up in her eyes as Beverly admitted how ashamed and embarrassed that made her feel, even in the midst of being thankful for their help.

"Dad's on another floor in this hospital. Eric said he was conscious throughout most of the rescue and was able to give a report to the police. It seems like Dad has several minor injuries like you, but they want to keep him for observation. His heart and his blood pressure had quite a shock, and the doctors want to monitor that due to the medical challenges he's had over the past year or two. Dad told the police that the speeding car crushed your car into a big parked truck. There was no one in the truck." Jennifer paused. "But Dad saw the paramedics cover the other driver, who died at the scene."

Beverly closed her eyes again at this tragic news. She had no idea who the driver was, this person who had hurt her so badly, and yet she was grieved at the news. She asked Jennifer to pray with her. Then Jennifer gently hugged her mother and thanked God for His protection of her parents. Beverly rested with Jennifer at her side, knowing her husband Leonard was being taken care of nearby.

When Eric had received the call last night that Leonard and Beverly Douglas had been in an accident, he prayed with his wife for a few minutes before leaving for the hospital. He called her an hour later to report the condition of her parents, just minor injuries and a possible concussion for her mom, who was still unconscious. The doctors also wanted to monitor Leonard since he wasn't in very good general health. Eric spent the late hours of the night and into the early morning with the doctors and the police officer who had taken Leonard's statement at the accident. The officer was Stanley, a young man from his church congregation who had joined the police force a few years ago. He was still new enough to be on the graveyard shift. Officer Stanley explained some of the accident procedures.

"Of course, their car is totaled. What the crash did not destroy, the rescue did. The firemen had to spray down the engine in order to give them time to extract your parents. They were wedged in there pretty tight. The firemen had to cut apart the metal frame."

"Was the car crumpled so badly?" asked Eric.

"It was pretty bad, but it seems that the firemen couldn't easily remove your parents because they are so...large."

"Oh." Eric understood.

"I was able to take Mr. Douglas's statement at the scene, and he gave a pretty good account of the situation. He said they were driving home from Thanksgiving dinner at your house, but that he had not been drinking." Officer Stanley paused to give Eric a chance to respond.

"That's true. I don't think I've ever seen that man drink." Eric confirmed what the officer was trying to verify.

"Mrs. Douglas was unconscious at the scene. And the other driver...never regained consciousness," said the officer sadly.

"Do you mean to say that he died in the crash?" asked Eric tentatively.

"No, the driver was a woman, and she died," explained the officer.

"Wow. What a night!" sighed Eric.

"It's been tragic, but unfortunately, as law enforcement officers we were warned to expect these things on Thanksgiving weekend. Do you know that this is one of the most fatal weekends of the year?

You would think family events would be joyful celebrations without the booze. But it seems like more alcohol gets consumed trying to get through a few hours with estranged family you only see once or twice a year. And then they storm out in a rage, driving off in their cars and right into accidents, hurting themselves and strangers. Or else, people are alone and so lonely they drink themselves numb before getting in their car. Tragic. This is also the busiest weekend for organ donations," explained Officer Stanley, shaking his head.

"So, do you think she was a drunk driver?" Eric asked.

"I don't know. Forensics will have to study the accident, and an autopsy might be done. Your parents will probably be advised if they want to take legal action."

"Legal action? I think we'll focus on other things for a while, like praising God my family is safe and looking for ways to minister to the other people involved," said Eric.

"Boy, the owner of the parked truck was sure upset. He hadn't had his truck very long, and now it's in bad shape, maybe a total loss. The whole back end was crumpled like a tin can, and the force might have bent the whole frame. If it had been any more jacked up, the Toyota could have slid right under it so that the bed would have smashed right into your folks' windshield," said Officer Stanley, shaking his head.

"Another thing to thank God for – a truck not too jacked up!" laughed Eric.

It was easy to find the location of the accident. This was a familiar stretch of road between Eric's house and the Douglas home, but he would never look at it the same way again. On the day after the accident, the smashed truck was still sitting by the curb, or rather, the back was precariously pressed against the curb while the front passenger tire was resting on top of the curb. Eric could see where the Douglas's Toyota had impacted with the tailgate. Thankfully, Eric remembered Officer Stanley's comment about the truck not being jacked up too high which prevented the Toyota from sliding under the tailgate to possibly inflict greater personal injury.

A young man was out looking at the truck, pacing and gesticulating while talking on his cell phone. Eric pulled over and parked. He thought this might be the truck owner and that he could probably use some encouragement. As Eric approached, the young man removed the phone from against his ear, pressed a button or two, and shoved it into the back pocket of his jeans.

"Is this your truck?" Eric asked in a friendly but sympathetic way.

"Yeah, for all of six months," the man groaned.

"It looks pretty bad, but is it totaled?"

"I don't think so. My insurance company is sending someone out to look at it. They have reps working this afternoon, the day after Thanksgiving, if you can believe that!" he explained in his surprise.

"I understand from my law enforcement friends that Thanksgiving is a pretty busy weekend for accidents and injuries. And my wife tells me it's busy for plumbers, too, with everyone stuffing potato peels down their kitchen sink, clogging their garbage disposal," Eric tried to cheer the young man. "By the way, it was my wife's parents in the car that was smashed into your truck. Unfortunately, the driver of the car that hit them died in the accident."

"Wow! That's tragic. It makes my truck problem seem small. How are your folks doing?" The young man looked genuinely concerned. After updating him about Beverly and Leonard's conditions, Eric offered to exchange contact information. The young man, Wayne Long, had just moved to town with his wife over the summer to serve out the remainder of his enlistment as the Marine recruiter in town. He planned to get his teaching degree in Physiology and Fitness, so he volunteered at the Youth Clubs of Albany as a sports coach and fitness instructor.

"I'm the son of a drill sergeant," explained Wayne jocularly, "so fitness is a part of my life." When Eric introduced himself, Wayne slapped the side of his head. "I recognize you now. My wife Cindy and I have visited your church a few times since we moved to town."

That gave Eric a great opportunity to personally invite Wayne and his wife back to church, and he extended an invitation to a family meal on Sunday afternoon on a date a few weeks after Christmas.

"I have a son and daughter-in-law about your age, and they would probably be happy to get to know a few more couples in this area. They can't always hang around their parents and grandparents. Chris and Ashley grew up here in Albany, so they can certainly show you around. Do you ever go over to the Marine base east of town?"

"Yes. Marine bases are familiar to us, and Cindy still goes to the commissary and the hospital for medical checkups since she's pregnant. She would probably appreciate a tour of Albany. Thanks for the invitation for lunch, too," said Wayne.

"I hope to see you before then, at church," said Eric as he walked away from the scene.

Chapter 4

The weeks between Thanksgiving and Christmas were spent shuttling between the Harvey and the Douglas home. Jennifer went to stay with her mom, who was released a few days after the accident. Beverly needed rest, so Jennifer served her mother while they tried to patiently wait for Leonard's release a few days later. Beverly was sitting up and walking around the house by the time Leonard came home, but she settled down for a few more days to be close to Leonard. Jennifer went home to her family but came over for several hours each day to keep up the house and make sure her parents were following the medical instructions.

When Leonard and Beverly felt ready to move around more, Hannah and Samuel came over to go on short walks with their grandparents. They were also ready to play games and work on jigsaw puzzles once they had a winter break from school.

Beverly was the type of person who did her Christmas shopping year-round and was a savvy on-line buyer as well. She did not feel anxious about having Christmas presents ready for her whole family, but she didn't think she would be up to all her baking and decorating activities during the holidays. Beverly's beautiful gourmet kitchen stayed tidy and clean with less activity than normal. Her bright pink appliances still looked cheery and inviting, but she knew she could not handle her usual baking projects. Perhaps she could find a reason to bake in a few months. Chris' wife Ashley was a big help wrapping up some of the final packages and helping Beverly decorate the house. While they worked together, Beverly was thrilled to give Ashley some decorations that she could use in her new home. Some ornaments came with a story about an incident when Chris was little. Beverly explained.

"Chris was such a cute toddler. He's several years older than his sister and brother, so he was an only child for a while, but his cousins would come around for Christmas. Eric's sister had kids a little older than Chris, but we didn't see them as much when they moved to California. My son Darren has two boys close to Chris' age. Sometimes I would take all three boys while their parents went out together, shopping and dining in the evenings, or serving someone in Eric's church during the day. Eric is kind of handy, but Darren has a lot of handyman skills, being in the construction business. They would make repairs for someone while the ladies would clean and bring meals and goodies. I usually had a lot of baked goods ready to donate for their good causes.

"Anyway," Beverly continued, "about these ornaments. I have this set of tiny figures from the Nativity that I like to hang on the tree. There is baby Jesus in a manger, Mary, Joseph, some animals, shepherds, wise men and an angel. Well, one of Darren's boys, Todd, told Chris that Grandma had baked these tiny cookies for decoration. I came out to see Chris with his cheeks stuffed with these ornaments!" Beverly and Ashley laughed at the thought. "I don't know if I have pictures of that or not, but you'll have to come over again, and we'll look for other pictures of Chris when he was little. So cute!"

A few nights later, Leonard and Beverly sat companionably in their den. "I heard the rescue team talking," Beverly admitted to Leonard.

"I wondered if you had," Leonard responded, waiting to hear what Beverly felt about the comments made by the rescue workers who couldn't get them out of their car because they were so fat.

"Pretty embarrassing, huh?" Beverly asked.

"Yes. I felt totally helpless, being trapped in my own car with you stuck so close to me but yet I couldn't reach you," Leonard admitted as he looked over at his beloved wife.

"We're fat," Beverly stated succinctly. "Too fat."

"Dangerously fat," Leonard retorted.

"We've been embarrassed before, but it hasn't motivated us to make any lasting changes," confessed Beverly.

"We've just had a big wake-up call, Bev. You know I hate to feel helpless for myself, and even more so when I can't help you. But even this feeling is not enough motivation. We've got to search our hearts and cry out to God for help because we don't know the right thing to do," implored Leonard.

"Let's do that together, honey," Beverly agreed as she reached out to hold Leonard's hand before they bowed their heads to pray together.

Beverly accompanied Leonard to his appointment. Or did Leonard accompany Beverly? They had made consecutive appointments with their family doctor for checkups ten days after the accident. They had both stayed in the hospital for a few days, Leonard two days longer, but they had been home together resting and recuperating for almost a week.

Before they had left for their appointment, they had looked each other over to see that most of the abrasions from the broken glass and air bags had healed. The doctor wanted to check on the more serious issues. For Beverly, he took a closer look at the large gash she had received on the side of her head, which was mending nicely. Since she had probably received a concussion, he checked her head and neck and interviewed her about dizziness, nausea and specific aches and pains. After careful consideration, she admitted that after resting at home for the past week, she was not still suffering in these areas. Beverly did not want to renew any prescriptions since she was only taking ibuprofen occasionally for minor pain. Leonard rejoiced that his wife had recovered so well.

They anticipated that Leonard's checkup would go as quickly and smoothly as Beverly's. After the doctor checked the abrasions and interviewed Leonard about any continuing aches and pains, he looked at Leonard's medical chart.

"I'm glad the hospital ran some additional tests on you, Leonard. Although you appeared to stay conscious and calm during the accident, the excitement certainly elevated your heart stress and blood pressure. We've been working to improve your general health over the past few years, but a trauma like this can really challenge a weak system like yours," the doctor warned.

"Doctor, we've known you a long time, and you've always done your best by Beverly and me. You have challenged us in the past to improve our health and watch our weight, but we've never seriously taken your advice. I've got to say that we certainly got a wake-up call from this accident," Leonard admitted.

"Well, being overweight certainly puts pressure on your heart and blood pressure. They were elevated at the scene, but I don't see any signs of apoplexy or coronary infarction from the accident," said the doctor as he looked at the test results again.

"What happened to us won't show up on the chart, doctor. I overheard something that night that I had hoped Beverly didn't hear, but she tells me she did. When the paramedics and firemen were planning how to rescue us, they could not get us out of our crumpled car because we were so fat. I felt so helpless and ashamed. It took us a few days at home before we could talk about it, but Beverly and I admit that we have a problem and want to start dealing with it immediately. Gyms and exercise videos all have a warning notice at the beginning to "consult your doctor before doing anything drastic like these exercises," so we thought we'd better talk to you about it now." Leonard looked over at Beverly who smiled in agreement with his comments to the doctor.

Leonard and Beverly continued to discuss with the doctor some education and programs for weight loss including diet and exercise. The doctor also cautioned them about the link between obesity and diabetes. As they drove home, they talked about some of the programs and gimmicks they had already invested in over the years. Gym memberships. Home gym equipment. Fad diets. Packaged food that tasted like packaged food. Meetings and clubs. It all added up to a lot of money without results. Something wasn't working.

"Honey, we have another resource that we've never really accessed when it comes to these issues," said Leonard, a bit mysteriously. Beverly could not guess what he was referring to, so he continued without further delay. "We believe God's Word is powerful and sufficient for every aspect of life, right? Don't you think God has something to say about our weight problems?"

"Yes, I do, dear. But I really don't know what," Beverly replied as she thought about what her husband had said.

"We could start looking in the Bible when we get home. I think we have to humble ourselves a little more. After admitting the problem to our doctor, we really need to talk to our pastor."

Chapter 5

Leonard and Beverly Douglas were members of Grace Community Church. The church was situated on a convenient plot of land with a few trees on the north side of the Liberty Expressway. Much to their granddaughter Hannah Harvey's delight, the Albany mall was not far away, so some people went over to hang out after church services. The church facilities, which Grace had inherited from an older Baptist congregation, easily accommodated 600 people in the main worship center, with plenty of classrooms for adult fellowship groups, youth classes, and nursery facilities. The large all-purpose room was the size of a gymnasium and provided a necessary interior play and gathering area for energetic activities year-round.

In addition to the main worship service at 9:00 a.m. every Sunday morning, there was a variety of classes at 10:30 for every age group. Many families returned on Sunday evening at 6:00 for another congregational worship service with a special children's service. Attendance in the evening service was higher on the first Sunday of the month when there was a potluck feast afterward. That was a special time of fellowship, but the best way to get to know people was to attend a home Bible study during the week. Whenever the Bible memory club for youth met on Wednesday nights, any adults who were not serving in the program could participate in other Bible study classes. There was ministry on every other day of the week, too, but it didn't always take place in the church building. Besides the home Bible studies, outreach groups visited neighbors, the sick and the elderly or reached out to children through hosting school Bible clubs and vacation Bible school programs.

Eric Harvey preached one message in the Sunday morning worship service and another message, more of an inductive Bible study class, on Sunday nights. There were other gifted men, elders and deacons, seminary-trained and lay believers, who led and taught the adult fellowship groups. Humble and enthusiastic women with hearts of service cared for and trained the children, showed hospitality, and gathered together to encourage other women to love God and their families. Service to the local church was an active part of the college and career group, and their fresh energy was a boost to the longtime teachers. Having a great team of servants and leaders allowed Eric plenty of Bible study time before tackling the administrative and pastoral responsibilities of this vibrant Christian church.

It had taken Eric several years to develop mentor relationships with the men who served on the elder board of the church. Thankfully they mentored him, too. There were still some challenges with a few old-timers who had "come with" the Baptist building and were used to doing things their own way. Eric continued to meet with them, listening to them before encouraging them to try to work with other believers in the church to do things God's way.

There were many special activities and events during the Christmas season, and Eric enjoyed all of them, as long as they focused on the reason for the season, the birth of Jesus Christ, the Son of God coming to earth to save people from their sins. Early in December, the children's ministry hosted a Saturday afternoon "party" for the children. It gave parents the opportunity to do some shopping, baking, or dating while the children practiced for the pageant they would perform a few weeks later. Rather than give up Sunday morning preaching from the Bible, the church held a potluck before the afternoon pageant on the third Sunday, although they did cancel the Sunday evening service that night. One of the most unusual activities that Grace Church sponsored was the gospel-preaching Santa Claus who made visits in the community with church members ready to give presents to orphans and sick children, and comfort to the old and infirm.

Nick Saint. This was his honest-to-goodness name. With a name like that, it was easy to wonder if he really was Santa Claus. Well, he was. Nick was a professional Santa Claus with his own set of whiskers. Since his dad was a professional Santa Claus before him, that might have had a bearing on the name choice. But the white hair and beard and pot belly were all his.

As a ministry, Nick liked to visit homeless shelters and nursing homes. His appearance gave him easy access to a lot of people. He made them smile. Several generous donors provided gifts to be distributed by any elves who could serve with him. While he was kind and patient with children who were amazed and confused about whether Santa was "real" or not, he always took the opportunity to tell people the true story about Jesus Christ, who was born, lived a perfect life, died on the cross to pay for the sins of anyone who would trust and believe in Him as Lord and Savior, and who rose again, victorious over sin and death. Nick had a special gospel message he attached to his candy canes, too. Other professional Santa gigs he did for the public didn't always allow him to talk about Jesus, but there were plenty of places that welcomed his ministry team with his jovial spirit, his generous gifts, and his message of hope.

For the rest of the year, Nick was a radio DJ on the local music and news station. He had a smooth voice and a cheerful tone. He liked talking in general, and talking with people over the radio or on the phone was almost as nice as face-to-face. With his particular appearance, as the old saying went, he had a good face for radio since he couldn't be seen. It was true that some DJs with great voices were not very good looking, so they did not match their suave voices. Since Nick always looked like Santa, it was easier to have an unseen job.

Nick kept up his appearance all year around, wearing red T-shirts or tropical print shirts besides keeping his beard in pristine white condition. After having it professionally bleached and processed years ago, he and his wife found it easier and more cost-efficient to take care of it at home. He kept his Santa waistline all year, too.

Some people were surprised that Nick and his wife Nadia kept their house in Christmas style all year around, too. It was something that brought them together, the colors and styles of the season brought joy to their family and friends any time of year. When their two daughters were teenagers, they felt embarrassed sometimes, but most of their friends enjoyed the novelty of seeing Santa at home. Now that their daughters were grown up, Nick looked forward to the day when his eldest daughter would place his first grandson in his arms for a picture with his Santa-styled grandpa.

Nick just hoped he would be around for many years to come. Nick's dad had died in his late 50s because of complications from diabetes, a disease that was complicated by his obesity. Nick was approaching that same age with the same waistline and the same warnings from his doctor about his health. He had always prided himself on being an authentic Santa – designer red suit and cap covering his own bushy white hair, his own silky white beard, and his own belly that shook like a bowl full of jelly. Yes, Nick wanted to play Santa and grandpa for a long time.

When Jennifer walked into her parents' home, she found her mom sitting at her kitchen table with the contents of her purse spread across the table top. The scene was shocking because her mom's kitchen was usually so clean and pristine. The junk was a jumbled mess with a few piles leaning precariously close to the edge.

"What's this, Mom? National Clean Out Your Purse Day? Let me take your picture and submit your entry to be the poster child," Jennifer teased her mother.

"I'm looking for something," mumbled Beverly, with her nose stuck in the tan leather handbag.

"It doesn't seem you could have anything else in that bag, Mom, unless you are Mary Poppins ready to extract a coat rack and a table lamp," replied Jennifer, before getting serious. "What are you looking for, Mom?"

"My membership card to the gym," Beverly explained.

"Well, here it is on the top of this pile of cards," said Jennifer as she picked up a stack of plastic cards. "Wait, this is a whole pile of membership cards to most of the gyms in town. And some diet centers, too. Mom, are you a member of all of the clubs and gyms?" Jennifer asked in amazement.

Beverly began to explain how every year when she made her New Year's resolution to lose weight, she and Leonard would check out the newest gym, fitness center, or diet meeting center in the area and join. But after a few weeks or months at the most, they would stop going, but kept paying for their membership, just in case.

Since it was still a few weeks before New Year's, Jennifer was concerned that her parents were about to continue this tradition and find a new gym to join. Before she had to lecture her mother about repeating this folly, Beverly explained what she was actually doing.

"After the accident, your father and I talked about the complications our obesity caused both in our rescue and our recovery. While our car was probably totaled anyway, it was a shame to require the fire department to chop our car apart to get us out. And the doctors warned your father and me that recovery from our injuries would be slow and painful because our bodies were already challenged by the burden of excess weight and stress on our hearts.

"But we're not going to join another gym," Beverly proclaimed. "Your father and I have been praying to God for wisdom and guidance. We want to deal with this problem God's way. After I cancel these memberships, we're going to meet with Eric, our pastor and beloved son-in-law, to get some counseling."

"Wow, Mom. It sounds like you are serious," said Jennifer as encouragingly as she could muster, even with her doubts. "But I don't think Eric has ever counseled anyone about these issues before."

"Maybe it's time he started addressing these issues, for our sakes as well as for others in the congregation. For now, your father and I need to address things in our own home, and we want to know what God says in the Bible about it, and Eric can certainly help."

"Can I help you cancel these memberships, Mom?" asked Jennifer.

"No thanks, honey. I got us into this mess, and I'm going to get us out. I'm keeping a log to tell your dad how much money we've spent on these memberships we've never used over the years. I'm sure we can think of better things to do with our money," Beverly laughed, but it sounded a bit like a discouraged sigh.

Chapter 6

If I believe that God's Word is sufficient to address every issue of life, then what does the Bible say about the obesity problem affecting my family?

Eric had been pondering this question for days, ever since Leonard and Beverly had sought his counsel. Their accident had given them a wake-up call not only about the physical and social problems caused by their weight but about spiritual issues as well. On this Monday morning in December, Eric looked at his calendar for the week and penciled in an hour each day to pray and search the Scriptures to answer this question. Eric relied on God's promise from 2 Peter 1:2-4 that said, "*His divine power has granted to us everything pertaining to life and godliness, through the true knowledge of Him who called us by His own glory and excellence.*" God's Word would point him to the right answers.

Eric began with prayer. *Dear Lord, You are a good and generous God. You have abundantly supplied all of my needs and the needs of my family. Thank You. But Leonard and Beverly are hurting. They are hurting with physical pain from the accident. They have been hurt by embarrassment and shame. Please continue to comfort them and heal them. But now they are aware that they have hurt You, Lord, by taking more of Your resources than they should and not being able to serve You because their physical bodies are weakened by obesity. They want to know, and I want to know, Lord, what You think about the issues surrounding obesity, what You have written in Your Word, and what Your will is for us in the days and years ahead. Teach me, O Lord, so that I can help Beverly and Leonard now, plus anyone in my congregation who will need help in the future. To God be the glory. Amen.*

While Eric knew he could easily research the topic of obesity online to discover the magnitude of this epidemic in the world today, he instead went to his most trusted guide for wisdom and perspective: his old Bible and trusty concordance. He trusted the Bible because he knew 2 Timothy 3:16-17 to be true, which said, *"All Scripture is inspired by God and profitable for teaching, for reproof, for correction, for training in righteousness; so that the man of God may be adequate, equipped for every good work."* First, he looked up the words *obesity* and *obese* in the concordance but found no use of these words in Scripture.

Next, he looked up the word *fat*. Here was a long list of this word used throughout the Old Testament, most of them references describing sacrifices and offerings. Of course, there was Pharaoh's dream about thin and fat cows at the end of Genesis along with the Old Testament story of Moab's King Eglon who got murdered with a sword that became stuck and hidden in his fat.

There were a few warnings to Israel about growing fat and forsaking God. That would be worth further consideration at a later time. Eric suspected that the issue wasn't about girth but rather that when people lived in abundance and indulged themselves, their sinful tendency was to forsake God and glorify themselves. His eyes fell on another word on this page: *fasting*. He might have to consider that later, but he wanted to stick to the issue at hand.

So far in his Monday study time, Eric had not picked any Bible vocabulary words from the concordance that would help him get a better understanding of this modern issue of obesity from a Biblical perspective. Was this not a problem in Bible times? Or was this not an issue that God addressed in the Bible? Or was it even a spiritual issue at all? Eric needed to analyze and understand the real issues at hand. *Obese* and *fat* were actually just labels describing the end result. So, what was the cause leading up to these results? Eric considered how someone became fat or obese. Eating. Eating too much. Eating more than your body needs to work. Indulgence. Not enough work for the body to burn the calories consumed. Laziness. This thought trail led Eric to think of one more word, a Bible word labeling a particular sin: gluttony.

Now wait a minute! When Eric imagined gluttony, his mind pictured drunken orgies with ridiculous amounts of food piled to overflowing on banquet tables, quantities being consumed with greasy hands by toga-wearing heathens before being unceremoniously expelled to make room for more. Was this what was happening in his home, family, and society?

Then Eric remembered the Thanksgiving spread in his own dining room last month, the night of the accident. He recalled his compliment to his wife about the abundance of food elaborately and beautifully displayed for their small group. He remembered enjoying a hearty meal with multiple servings, then lounging around watching the games on TV with desserts brought to his side. This pattern had been a family tradition for years. Was there something wrong with this?

OK, God. My previous focus on Beverly and Leonard's obesity was misdirected. I need Your perspective on gluttony, what it is and whom it has affected. This includes me.

Eric found only six verses in the Bible with some form of the word gluttony: Deuteronomy 21:20; Proverbs 23:20-21; Proverbs 28:7; Matthew 11:18-19; Luke 7:33-34; and Titus 1:12. At first glance, these verses did not seem to reveal much. It seemed that gluttony was usually linked with other evils such as heavy drinking and laziness, just like Eric had imagined. In the gospels, Jesus' own critics had accused Him of being a glutton, suggesting overindulgence, but the Hebrew word better described someone with an appetite simply being refreshed. As Eric looked at the various Hebrew words used in these verses for glutton, another associated concept came out – satisfaction. While it was one thing to someone to eat and satisfy their hungry stomach, it was another issue for them to try to satisfy their heart, or their spiritual soul, with food.

So, Eric decided to proceed with his studies by separating the sin issue of gluttony from the results of overeating and under-exercising that led to obesity and its related complications. It seemed to Eric that sticking to gluttony would not necessarily make it easier to talk about with his family and his congregation. And yet, God gave a clear framework for this communication through Scripture, for a pastor and fellow Christian to speak the truth in love about sin with other believers. If Eric could clearly identify the gluttony problem as a sin problem, then God's Word held the information and power to put off, or mortify, the sin as well as the forgiveness and restored peace that comes from true repentance. Eric felt challenged to begin treating gluttony like the sin that it was, no longer mocking and laughing at it like a human foible, or ignoring it as too personal. Then God could use him to help his family and congregation.

Eric decided to begin his personal evaluation by checking some of his recent eating experiences and making notes over the next few meals. Since the big Thanksgiving meal from last month was fresh in his mind, he would begin by asking himself some questions about that eating extravaganza.

What happened? What did I actually do? What did I actually eat? Eric remembered the beautiful warm room with the dining table spread with so many dishes of savory food. He thought of his first plate of food that he devoured right after the family prayer. On that plate, he had a generous serving of the traditional fare: turkey, stuffing, mashed potatoes with gravy, both kinds of cranberry and a few vegetables for color. He had eaten that while talking and laughing around the table with his family. It was a happy memory for Eric because it was a joyful family scene full of tradition and thankfulness.

Then Eric pictured his second plate of food for dinner, piled high with smaller servings of all the many different side dishes. He hadn't talked so much while he was eating then except to rave about the good tastes in his mouth. He remembered that his stomach felt full, but he ignored that feeling to finish his goal of cleaning that plate, too.

By the time the football game viewing began an hour later, Eric was stretched out in the recliner with his father-in-law and two sons in the den, his belt loose and a plate full of desserts at his elbow.

Somehow those goodies disappeared. Did he even remember tasting and enjoying them? Not really, he had to admit. He knew he had eaten the equivalent of another full meal later that evening when he snacked in the kitchen with Jennifer after the dinner party. It was a fun time for the two of them as they shared and laughed about the highlights of their family celebration. It was also a time of peace and quiet with his wife, just hours before he got the call about the car accident that would agitate the midnight hours for them.

What was I thinking at the time? What do I think about it now? Eric remembered feeling thankful for his family and the abundant food that evening. He thought of the satisfaction and security knowing that his family had a lovely home with such abundance. He remembered thinking that there was so much food prepared, way more than his little family could possibly need or eat, such a large quantity for a small group of people. Eric sensed all the food was delicious, enjoying the savory dishes of the season. Thinking back, Eric knew that he had done a lot of eating without even thinking about or appreciating what he was doing. He also remembered his conscious effort to suppress his stomach's signal that he was full so that he could continue his consuming activities. An honest assessment now, weeks after the event, required Eric to admit that he had eaten way more food that his body required. He had acted as a glutton, overeating to glorify and please himself.

Looking back at his written answers to these questions, Eric noticed words and phrases that surprised him. He circled anything that he had written that seemed sinful and tried to identify it clearly with a biblical word. From this analysis, he wrote a list of the sinful thoughts and actions he had identified. *Selfish. Greedy. Indulging his senses. Suppressing his conscience. Laziness. Pride.* His heart began to ache as he knelt to pray and ask the Lord's forgiveness for these sins that he committed. This was not just an issue for him to address with others, but this was personal.

Joy. Eric was reminded again of the joy of his salvation after mourning over his sin and being forgiven. *Hope.* Eric also knew that God's Word would contain hope of how to fight off these sins in the future. He turned back to his list of sinful thoughts and deeds and challenged himself to figure out the "antidote." What did God's Word tell believers to put on in place of sin that they had put off? Putting this plan together would give him wisdom to avoid sin when faced with these food temptations in the future. Before his time of personal examination was over, Eric prayed again, thanking God for revealing so much truth about the battle against the sin of gluttony.

Later that night, Eric stumbled out of bed to the kitchen for a drink of water. In the shadows, he was startled to almost trip on one of Samuel's elephant figurines in the living room. Even on a dark night, there was no mistaking the shape of that elephant as he picked it up and put it safely on the table. Eric knew the African animal report had become a large project, with plans to construct a large papier-mâché creature. What would they do with an elephant in their living room for a few months until the end of the school year? And after Samuel displayed it for his school report, where would his craft reside after that?

"There is obviously an elephant in my living room," Eric announced in the still of the night to no one in particular. Hearing this truth made him think of an old English idiom. "There's an elephant in the room," he stated plainly. The idiom was based on the idea that an elephant in the room would be impossible to overlook. The elephant was an obvious truth that was either being ignored or going unaddressed. If people came into the room and pretended the elephant wasn't there, they were choosing to avoid dealing with a looming problem. Like gluttony.

Eric remembered an old comedy routine by Jimmy Durante, who would walk down the street leading an elephant. When a police officer questioned him, "What are you doing with that elephant?" Durante would reply, "What elephant?" The crowd always laughed.

Gluttony was a controversial issue. It's something that everyone is aware of because the results are usually displayed by a body ranging from chubby to obese. Eric knew from experience that talking about overeating caused great embarrassment and could trigger emotional or even violent reactions. While it ought to be discussed openly, it was hard to do. But Eric also knew that this issue was not going away by itself and that the culture in which they lived would not provide any solutions. People were suffering from the sin and its natural health consequences. At the root of gluttony was sin. So, it was a spiritual issue that God was willing to deal with.

As a pastor, Eric needed to confront sin issues. He needed to bring wisdom about this issue of gluttony to his family and his congregation. He needed to speak the truth in love because so many people were hurting from this sin and its consequences. Before Eric returned to bed, he wrote himself a note promising to address this issue soon with the people he loved.

Chapter 7

Sunday, January 4 dawned bright but cold in Albany, Georgia. On this morning, Eric Harvey's family was ready to go early so that they could all drive together to church. While others opened the church building and made the facilities ready for the activities of the day, Eric and a group of men gathered to pray. On this particular morning, just like every other Sunday, they prayed to God that the message from the Bible would be clear and accurate, representing the one true God in spirit and truth and that it would be well-received by believers to apply to their Christian walk, and by unbelievers to lead to their salvation. The elders knew that today's message would be challenging for many, so they prayed for extra grace for those who might feel hurt or confused, or who might react with open hostility.

Worship time began with more prayer, a variety of hymns and spiritual songs sung by the choir and congregation, general announcements and Scripture reading. Eric read Psalm 32 from his New American Standard Bible.

"A Psalm of David. A Maskil. How blessed is he whose transgression is forgiven, whose sin is covered! How blessed is the man to whom the Lord does not impute iniquity, and in whose spirit there is no deceit!

"When I kept silent about my sin, my body wasted away through my groaning all day long. For day and night Your hand was heavy upon me; my vitality was drained away as with the fever heat of summer. Selah. I acknowledged my sin to You, and my iniquity I did not hide; I said, 'I will

confess my transgressions to the Lord'; and You forgave the guilt of my sin. Selah.

"Therefore, let everyone who is godly pray to You in a time when You may be found; surely in a flood of great waters they will not reach Him. You are my hiding place; You preserve me from trouble; You surround me with songs of deliverance. Selah. I will instruct you and teach you in the way which you should go; I will counsel you with My eye upon you. Do not be as the horse or as the mule which have no understanding, whose trappings include bit and bridle to hold them in check, otherwise they will not come near to you.

"Many are the sorrows of the wicked, but he who trusts in the Lord, lovingkindness shall surround him. Be glad in the Lord and rejoice, you righteous ones; and shout for joy, all you who are upright in heart."

Another prayer was spoken before another hymn was sung, then Eric stood up and buttoned his suit jacket before taking his place behind the pulpit to begin his first sermon of the new year.

"Beloved friends, we will be studying Psalm 32 this morning and applying it to a very specific area of our Christian lives. I have been challenged in recent weeks to use this passage to examine my own life, seek forgiveness for sin, and look for practical applications and changes that God would want me to make in my daily walk.

"How many of us have made resolutions for the New Year?" Eric paused to watch many people raise their hands. "We seem to be a regular group of Americans. Statistics report that approximately 45% of Americans make New Year's resolutions. History shows people making resolutions going back to the Babylonians and Romans. Medieval knights took an annual "peacock vow" to chivalry. In church history, we see the annual Catholic Lent tradition and the Methodist Watch Night. A resolution is supposed to be a promise, something you say you are going to do before doing it. In the case of New Year's resolutions, though, these promises are better described as wishes and goals of self-improvement over the next year.

"We are too big of a congregation for you to shout out what areas of your life you made resolutions about, but I expect that the general public statistical reports are probably pretty accurate about the areas of self-improvement we might wish to change. People want to improve in the areas of family and personal relationships, financial and time management, to quit bad habits like smoking or heavy drinking, to increase their education, or to volunteer or do other good deeds. But the most common and highest ranking resolution always addresses weight loss and fitness. On the one side, the issue is changing the habit of overeating. On the other side, it is the problem of the lack of activity and exercise to burn the fuel calories ingested.

"It's no wonder that people in general and Americans in particular see the need to make improvements in this area. Statistics reveal that 66% of adult Americans are considered overweight. More drastic is the fact that 33% are clinically obese.

"Americans are making good resolutions, but they are failing to keep them. They see that they have a problem, but they can't seem to do anything about it. On the contrary, the statistics are getting worse every year about the number of people overweight and the excess of weight per person. There have been many studies to determine why people fail to accomplish their New Year's resolutions. These reasons include the fact that resolutions were made with unrealistic or unclear goals that were not or could not be measured or tracked. People admitted to forgetting their own resolutions or to being confused because they made too many. The bottom line about failing to keep their resolutions is this: people took no direct action; they did nothing about them.

"Now, wait a minute. Think about the gym memberships purchased in January," Eric chided as the congregation nodded in knowing agreement. "Or the equipment sitting unused in your basement or garage." The congregation chuckled because they knew it was true in their own houses. "And now there are a plethora of gadgets and apps that are available on every mobile device. But in the same way that just making a resolution doesn't change anything, neither does buying the membership, the equipment or the gadgets.

"There is a huge disconnect between knowledge and action. Americans know that they have a problem. They know that health and fitness are important to their quality of life. Americans would say that being healthy is a good thing. They have expressed this knowledge about the right thing in a variety of ways, most clearly seen in these annual New Year's resolutions. But they keep making the same resolutions each January because they have taken no action to deal with them in the last twelve months.

"Instead, the world seems to deal with the problem of overeating and obesity in three ways. First, the world makes it acceptable. Obesity has been labeled and excused as a disease to allow it to be acceptable and tolerated. In another strategy, obesity has become a normal theme of humor. Those who had been bullied by others who also laughed at them have turned the tables by joking and laughing first, not only in the schoolyard but on comedy stages and feature films. And then there is the attempt to just ignore the problem. It has become easy in our society to accommodate a large person without any fanfare. The problem of overeating has become, like the old saying goes, an elephant in the room. Everyone knows the problem is there, it's so big, but everyone tries to pretend it's not really there at all.

"But, dear friends, I have been challenged recently to look at the problem of overeating and all of its ramifications in the light of Scripture, God's Word. What does God think about the obesity epidemic in our country, and even in our churches? Does God's Word address not only the problem but the solution? Is this a spiritual issue? I have found that God's Word does, in fact, address this issue.

"As I said before, the average American knows and admits that overeating is not good, that being overweight is unhealthy, that obesity is a problem. We know the right thing to do is eat less and exercise more. Please listen to what God says in James 4:17: '*Therefore, to the one who knows the right thing to do and does not do it, to him it is sin.*' That's right, our problem of overeating is a sin problem.

"I think it's important to clearly identify the sin problem using Biblical terms rather than worldly labels. The word obesity is not in the Bible. Obesity is an extreme symptom and result of overeating. The word fat appears numerous times in the Old Testament referring to the substance on the animals that were to be sacrificed. There is only one man described in the Bible as fat. In Judges 3 you can read the story of the King of Moab, named Eglon, who was murdered with a sword that became hidden in his rolls of fat. So, what is this Bible word that we can and should use to identify the sin of overeating?

"Gluttony. To me, this is a word that causes me to cringe. It carries with it the images of pagan orgies with ancient Greeks wearing togas and laying around eating greasy meat with their hands while young maidens drop grapes into their mouths before getting up to dance. So, with this caricature in mind, we might not think gluttony is what we're doing. But I actually think that it will be helpful to use the word gluttony to identify this sin, especially when we understand an accurate definition of the word and compare it to our actions. The word glutton appears only five or six times in all of Scripture. A person who is identified as a glutton is often also identified as being a drunkard or with a drunkard, as in Deuteronomy 21:20. The father in Proverbs gives warnings to his son not to be a glutton or drunkard nor to associate with them because it will lead to poverty and humiliation, as in Proverbs 23:20-21 and Proverbs 28:7. In Titus 1, Cretans were insultingly identified as liars, evil beasts, and lazy gluttons.

"But did you know that Jesus was accused of being a glutton? Let's look at Luke 7. There is a parallel account in Matthew 11:18-19, but please turn to Luke 7, verses 33-34. Jesus is responding to a group of Pharisees when He says, *'For John the Baptist has come eating no bread and drinking no wine, and you say, 'He has a demon!' The Son of Man has come eating and drinking, and you say, 'Behold, a gluttonous man and a drunkard, a friend of tax collectors and sinners!'* We know that Jesus was a human being, and He ate food to satisfy His needs. But these were accusations of gluttony!

"This would be a good time to clearly define gluttony. We have already linked gluttony with overeating, but it would behoove us to get very specific when we identify this problem because we want to be able to look through Scripture to find God's solution. Please consider both parts of this definition: The sin of gluttony is eating too much food, and eating food for the wrong reason. Let me say it again: The sin of gluttony is eating too much food, and eating food for the wrong reason.

"Now folks, this was just my introduction to the message I want to bring you now from God's word. I've laid out the statistics. I've told you the bad news, and for many of us, what you have just heard is an exhortation against you that you have a sin problem, the specific sin of gluttony. That is the bad news. You should be sad and remorseful about your sin. But I don't want to leave you there, wallowing in that sadness or self-pity. We have to truly identify this problem as sin so that we can deal with it the way God has provided. Yes, we have sinned. But yes, we have hope. First John 1:9 says, *'If we confess our sins, He is faithful and righteous to forgive us our sins and to cleanse us from all unrighteousness.'* Please notice in this single verse the elements of confession, forgiveness, and cleansing. This is God's way of dealing with sin.

King David, a man after God's own heart, committed gross sins when he committed adultery with Bathsheba then had her husband murdered. After a year of wallowing in his guilt without repenting, God sent the prophet Nathan to confront David about his sin. When David truly repented, he penned Psalm 32. In this beautiful poem, we see God's plan of confession, forgiveness, and cleansing expanded and explained. Let's look at it again in detail.

"Here is the outline we will use as we examine this Psalm for the next few minutes. In verses one and two, we see God's hope. In verses three through five, we hear confession. Then in verses six through nine, we follow the action of dealing with sin. Finally, David closes this Psalm with joy that comes when sin has been dealt with God's way.

"So let's read again verses one and two to see God's hope. *'A Psalm of David. A Maskil. How blessed is he whose transgression is forgiven, whose sin is covered! How blessed is the man to whom the Lord does not impute iniquity, and in whose spirit there is no deceit!'* The blessings that are offered are to sinners who are forgiven because their sin is covered by Jesus' atoning blood. It is a blessing that God no longer imputes or places the blame for iniquity to man, but rather, when God imputed or credited our sins to Christ at His death, God was able to attribute Jesus' righteousness to every believer.

"There is hope for believers when they deal with their sin by seeking God's forgiveness. This might be a hard message to listen to because our weight is such a personal topic. Talking about it may hurt, but God's message dealing with any sin begins with hope and ends with joy.

"Let's move on to verses three through five where we hear about confession. *'When I kept silent about my sin, my body wasted away through my groaning all day long. For day and night Your hand was heavy upon me; my vitality was drained away as with the fever heat of summer. Selah. I acknowledged my sin to You, and my iniquity I did not hide; I said, "I will confess my transgressions to the Lord"; and You forgave the guilt of my sin. Selah.'*

"In David's situation at this point in history, we can read what happened in 2 Samuel 11 and 12. It appears that David suffered physically over the course of time from when he first took Bathsheba until after the baby was born and Nathan confronted him. One of the physical penalties of the sin of gluttony is not the wasting away of the body like David experienced, but rather the enlargement of the body, yet with a similar drain on vitality that David describes in verses three and four. The word *selah* after these two thoughts indicates some kind of pause, perhaps even a musical interlude, but it is a stopping point to think about the idea that was just expressed.

"After considering what might happen to a Christian physically after sin has been committed but confession is delayed, we read in verse five what happens when a Christian confesses and truly repents of his sin. God forgives sin.

"What is confession? The word means to say the same thing as God. Confession involves correctly identifying sin and telling the truth about how bad it is, how much it offends a holy and righteous God. That's why I wanted to find and use the Bible word of gluttony to correctly identify the sin that has been occurring. As Americans, we have the knowledge that overeating is not a good habit for our physical health. We are not good stewards of the bodies that God has given us. We are eating too much food, and we're eating food for the wrong reasons. Obesity is one glaring result of gluttony, but there are plenty of others. Some consequences may not be so obviously visual, such as other eating disorders or diseases such as diabetes or high blood pressure. There are both personal and social consequences.

"The end of verse five ends with describing some attributes of God: forgiveness and mercy. God keeps His promises to believers to forgive their sins.

"In the next few verses, we see David's poetic description of dealing with sin on a continuing basis, also known as sanctification. In New Testament terms, we deal with sin by putting off the sinful thoughts, words, and deeds and replacing them by putting on righteousness that fits into those circumstances. Let's read those verses again now, verses six through nine: *'Therefore, let everyone who is godly pray to You in a time when You may be found; surely in a flood of great waters they will not reach Him. You are my hiding place; You preserve me from trouble; You surround me with songs of deliverance. Selah. I will instruct you and teach you in the way which you should go; I will counsel you with My eye upon you. Do not be as the horse or as the mule which have no understanding, whose trappings include bit and bridle to hold them in check, otherwise they will not come near to you.'*

"Let me just point out some of the features from these verses: prayer in verse six; taking refuge in God in verse seven; receiving God's instructions, teaching and counsel from His written Word; and a warning against rebellion.

"Finally I want you to see that if we truly confess and repent of our sins, there is joy. Verses ten and eleven say, *'Many are the sorrows of the wicked, but he who trusts in the Lord, lovingkindness shall surround him. Be glad in the Lord and rejoice, you righteous ones; and shout for joy, all you who are upright in heart.'*

"In contrast to the sorrows of the wicked, those believers who have sinned, then confessed and repented, are surrounded with His lovingkindness. We can be glad, rejoice and shout for joy. Psalm

51:12 says it this way, '*Restore to me the joy of Your salvation and sustain me with a willing spirit.*'

"If we correctly identify our sin as sin, God has clearly told us how to deal with sin. If we seriously deal with sin according to God's instructions, then we will receive forgiveness and the joy of our salvation. God addresses the issue of what to do when Christians sin. At the moment of salvation, we were forgiven for all our sins, past, present and future. But then Christians are called to work out their salvation with fear and trembling, dealing with sin that might encumber us but will never enslave us again.

"Please note, dear people in the congregation listening to me today, that this hope and confession and sanctification and joy is God's plan for Christians. If you feel powerless to understand this issue, and you cannot tell the truth about these issues to yourself or God in confession, and if you cannot or will not put off sin and put on righteousness, and if you feel no hope or joy, then you may not be a Christian. You may not have made the most important confession of all, to confess that Jesus Christ is the Lord and your Savior. You may not have known or believed Jesus' true story of being God, taking on the form of a man when He was born in Bethlehem so long ago, living a perfect life, dying on the cross to pay the penalty of other people's sins, rising again victorious over sin and death, and ascending to heaven where He rules forever. If you have any questions about how you can know Jesus as your Lord and Savior, please stop by our prayer room after the sermon this morning to talk to someone about salvation.

"For those of us believers whose consciences have been pricked about the sin of gluttony, I invite you to confess and repent of your personal sins. There is no way in one sermon that I can map out everything that God's Word has to say about putting off the sin of gluttony and everything that we can put on in righteousness. And you may have questions or comments in response to God's Word and this sermon. If so, please take a few moments to fill out the special yellow card that was included in your church bulletin. You can write your questions or comments on the back, or just indicate that you will prayerfully consider what you heard this morning. The elders have been discussing ways that we can come alongside one another as we try to apply God's truth to our lives. If you would be interested in gathering for some Biblical counseling for this issue, please mark your interest, and we will follow up with you in the next few weeks. Please drop those cards in the collection boxes by the doors as you leave today, or in the offering baskets in the next few weeks.

"As we close the sermon today, I want to give you the greeting of Happy New Year. May that happiness be joy from the Lord that comes from obedience and true repentance. Let's pray."

Chapter 8

Although Eric and Jennifer were not dressed incognito, they stood at the side of the foyer like the movie star characters in *Singing in the Rain* who were disguised in raincoats while they overheard the audience's comments after a preview of their first talking movie.

The first wave of comments came bursting noisily through the doors along with the hostile commentators who wanted to leave church quickly before anyone could, they feared, attack them more personally.

"We shouldn't be talking about this at church."

"I am so offended by this personal attack."

"Eating is not a sin."

"Doesn't the pastor care how bad I feel about my weight?"

"I would change my weight if I could, but I can't."

"I'm proud of my big body, and I don't care what anyone else says."

"God doesn't want me to seek after glamor and vanity."

"How I eat is none of his business."

"Just because I'm overweight does not mean I have a sin problem."

"There's nothing wrong with me just because I'm big."

"God loves me just the way I am, so why is this pastor picking on me?"

Eric had braced himself for emotional criticism from hurt or offended people in his congregation. He listened carefully to these reactions in order to prepare himself to minister to each of them as soon as the Lord gave him the opportunity. But Eric didn't see what came next. Literally. From around the corner of the atrium, Stan Merriwether barreled toward Eric with his little wife Betsy in tow. Before he came to a complete stop, Stan's finger was jabbing into Eric's shoulder as he raised his voice for everyone to hear.

"How could you be so cruel? Who do you think you are? Are you the fashion police? You're certainly not a medical doctor. You don't know what it's like to be big. You have no idea what goes on in people's homes or minds when they are eating a meal. And you say you're teaching from the Bible? My Bible doesn't invade someone's home and insult them. My Bible is full of feasts and gatherings in the tabernacle to worship God. What kind of pastor are you, attacking this congregation?" Stan labored to catch his breath from his heated speech after his full-speed march. It gave Eric the opportunity to move back from this raving man with a sharp tongue and sharp finger.

"Stan, let's sit down over here to the side. I'd like to hear what you have to say," Eric said as calmly as he could.

"Oh, you're going to hear me all right. But I want everyone to know that I think you've overstepped the bounds of your job as preacher and pastor. You were cruel and heartless in your attack of people who struggle with their weight. Just because we're big doesn't mean we're bigger sinners than you. You have no idea what you're talking about. I'll be talking to the elders this week about your unkind and unbiblical attack on me!" Having barely caught his breath from his first tirade, Stan stormed out of the lobby with his little wife Betsy timidly following in his wake.

Giselle did not storm out of the sanctuary like some of the other large people who were offended by Pastor Eric's sermon about the sin of gluttony. She did not admit to herself that she was angry. Rather, she tossed her thick auburn mane of hair defiantly as she chose to ignore his comments. She smiled and laughed with her group of friends who lingered after church before deciding on a place to meet for lunch.

Once the gang had gathered at the trendy sandwich deli and ordered meals of various sizes, she let her feelings be known.

"I'm sure other people struggle with sin, but I don't have a problem with food. I love food," she stated confidently, waving her hands over an overflowing lunch tray. "I may be heavier than all of you, but that doesn't stop me from doing what I want in life. I'm happy with this big body that God has given me."

The young crowd of friends was a little surprised by Giselle's pronouncement.

"I wonder if you've missed the point of the sermon, Giselle," her friend Sarah suggested. "Pastor Eric used Scripture to point out an area of sin that we may not have considered: our sinful motivations behind how much we eat and why we eat. He wasn't promoting a certain body image or recommending the monastic lifestyle. Personally, I need some time to think and pray about things on my own before I talk to my mom about it. I signed up for the Biblical counseling, too. I'm sure that God will show me if I need to change," Sarah said humbly.

"I don't need to change," Giselle stated flatly. But she would be watching the changes around church over the next few months.

The elders gathered for a quick meeting after church. "I'm sure Stan is not the only person who was hurt or challenged by your message today, Pastor Eric. We heard several people's immediate reactions to your sermon. We should follow up with them after they have a few days to think about it. We should also check around for reactions from the folks who tend to be quieter. We don't want anyone who is angry or miserable inside turning away from getting help," the church elder Bill Sanderson summed up.

"Yes. I understand some initial reactions will be anger or embarrassment or denial because they feel personally attacked about their size and weight." Eric remembered the comments he had overheard. "But remember, gentlemen, this issue is not about size; it's about sin. There are many of us who have been living with this sin, but it hasn't dramatically affected our waistline or health, yet. And there will be others who have suffered the effects of long-term overeating that are humble enough to respond to this exhortation even after just one sermon. There will be a balance between exhorting sinners and strengthening the weak. And this might also be a sin that someone attending our church loves more than God, so while we're exhorting some believers to deal with sin in the context of sanctification, we may also be challenging some to repent and believe unto salvation."

The elders nodded. After prayer, they gathered their Bibles, wives and children to head home for lunch, probably a lighter lunch after that sermon. Eric looked around for his family. He saw Hannah and Samuel carrying the collection boxes into his office. When he got to the doorway, he was surprised to see Jennifer standing behind his desk.

"I'm sorry, honey. We didn't know we would be making such a big pile." Jennifer looked up from the scattered yellow cards covering the surface of Eric's desk.

"What's all this?" Eric asked.

"These are the response cards from your message today, Dad," chimed in Samuel.

"You will have to look through them when you get home, Eric. It looks like several people wrote comments, some angry and critical to be sure. But most of what I've seen have been grateful and humble responses of repentance and requests for help."

As the Harvey family was leaving Eric's office, they passed through the foyer again. They were surprised to see one young lady sitting to the side, her eyes a bit puffy from crying and a tissue still gripped in her hand. After signaling to the children to head out to the car, Eric grabbed Jennifer's hand so that they could approach her as a united and friendly team.

"Hello, Stephany," Eric greeted. "It's been an emotional morning for some people. How are you doing?"

"Hello, Pastor Eric. Hi, Jennifer." Stephany Goodacre tried to smile. "Pastor, I was overwhelmed by what you said today. I've never heard anyone preach about being fat."

"Please be careful, Stephany. Eric was preaching about gluttony, and it often results in being fat," corrected Jennifer.

"Yes. I understand the difference, but I'm not used to the terminology, I guess." Stephany continued, "I've been going to churches my whole life, and most of them have been filled with fat...I mean, large people. It's almost like it's culturally acceptable here in the South and in churches here. No one has ever mentioned gluttony in my churches before."

"I don't know that many preachers talk about gluttony, but God certainly addresses it in the Bible, doesn't He?" Eric asked.

"Yes, but I've always kind of thought about overeating as a bad habit since it's not really hurting anybody else," answered Stephany.

"I was thinking about that very issue the other day, Stephany, and I realized that one person's overeating does affect many people," Eric replied.

"How?"

"Well, first, the extra food that you eat means that someone else didn't get to eat it, perhaps someone who really needed it."

"So because I bought it someone else couldn't have it?" Stephany asked thoughtfully.

"Yes, although probably more indirectly than that. We don't have food shortages at the grocery store, but the extra food you don't need could make a good meal for someone else who does need it. Another way it affects others is by medical treatment required for the consequential health issues like heart attacks and diabetes. That means rising health care costs for everyone. And our personal testimony could be hampered, too," said Eric, adding a spiritual element.

"What do you mean by that?" Stephany wanted to know.

"It could play out in a few ways. Perhaps a large person would miss out on a missionary trip because their health could not handle the rigors of the trip. Or perhaps when a large person is warning someone to repent they might seem hypocritical for not dealing with their own sins. Now I'm not saying we have to be perfect before we reach out with the gospel, but it can hamper our testimony."

"I've never thought about it that way," Stephany responded. "You know I have tried to deal with my weight, but nothing has helped. What should I do?"

"Well, Stephany, let's stop and praise the Lord that the truth of His Word has penetrated your heart today," rejoiced Eric. "Then let's keep in touch so that you can participate in some of the activities we're going to put together around here to help and encourage those who want to do battle with the sin of gluttony. We'll do it together and trust the Lord for the results."

Chapter 9

"I am so offended by this personal attack. Who does this pastor think he is, calling me fat and gluttonous in front of the church? He has no idea how I suffer. I don't like being fat, but I sure don't like being insulted about it either. I don't want to hear criticism like this at church. He should be trying to make me feel good."

Karen mumbled some of these thoughts as she stormed out of the church building after Pastor Eric's sermon about the sin of gluttony. She had only been attending this church for a few months at the invitation of a friend from work, but now she had no intention of coming again to be insulted and ridiculed. Normally she and her friend Beth went to lunch after church, but today she was almost to her car when Beth caught up with her.

"Hey, Karen. Wait up!" Elizabeth, who was overweight herself, was breathing heavily by the time she reached Karen's car. "Don't run off yet. Aren't we still getting together for lunch like we usually do?"

"How can you think about food after that sermon?" Karen bellowed. She was so mad at Pastor Eric that she didn't know if she wanted to starve herself or binge into oblivion to teach that meddling pastor not to criticize. Crazy ideas about revenge with food began to invade her mind. She brushed those revengeful plots and devious schemes to the side of her mind in order to release her wrath on Elizabeth. "I'm going home. Thanks a lot for inviting me to your church,

Elizabeth. I didn't realize you brought me to church to gang up on me with your goody-goody friends. And you're certainly not in any position to be casting aspersions about being fat!"

"Ouch. That hurt. But you're right on that point at least. How can I hope to show you the love and goodness of Jesus Christ when my testimony for Him is layered in this fat?" she said, indicating her plump form.

"Is this the kind of thing you usually talk about at church? I came with you because I thought we were friends. I thought this was going to be a place to feel safe and loved no matter what I did. I thought sermons were supposed to make you feel good, not ashamed," moaned Karen, with less venom towards Elizabeth and more truth revealing her heartache.

"Karen, let's go someplace and talk. This has been a challenging sermon for me too, but I hope I can set the record straight on a few things. Maybe instead of lunch right now, we take a walk in the park. It's a nice day, and I'd really hate to see you go away mad without getting things straightened out." Karen reluctantly agreed to go to the park with Elizabeth.

When they were strolling along the winding path around the park lake, Elizabeth began to explain her situation. "You know, Karen, I've been in some churches that are like what you described earlier. Acquaintances put on a happy face to get together for an hour, someone stands in front to tell you that God loves you just the way you are, then you leave feeling good because you did church for the week. My mom and dad took me to a different kind of church when I was young, one that lovingly but truthfully confronted sin and presented God's plan for repentance, forgiveness, and transformation by following Christ. It's been hard to find another church like it since I've been on my own, but I think I've found the right people here at Grace Community. My folks taught me that church wasn't about me; it's about worshipping God. Part of worshipping God together with other people is to study the Bible, learn what it means and apply it to our lives. If we study it together, then we have a group to help us while we're trying to practice obeying God's commands."

"Obeying God's commands? Why would you want someone else telling you what to do? We're independent. I thought God loved us and was here to help us have a good life," pondered Karen.

"God does love us, Karen, but He's not simply a benevolent grandfather giving us whatever we want whenever we want it. I have one of those, a benevolent grandfather, and as much as I love him and know that he loves me, sometimes when he has spoiled me it's left me sick, miserable, and ungrateful." The two ladies chuckled together, shaking their heads at the memories of being overindulged.

"God loves us so much that He doesn't just give us what we think is best, because we're often wrong, aren't we? But He offers us what He knows is best because He created all things. You've probably heard this familiar verse even in some of those wishy-washy church experiences. John 3:16: *'For God so loved the world that He gave His only begotten Son that whoever believes in Him shall not perish but have everlasting life.'*"

"I don't see how Jesus has anything to do with the food that I eat," argued Karen.

"Stay with me on this, Karen," explained Elizabeth. "God loved us by sending us a Savior, Jesus Christ. That's really good news only when you understand the bad news." Elizabeth paused, hoping Karen would ask the right question. She did.

"So what's the bad news?"

"The bad news for me is that I am a sinner who has offended a perfectly holy God who created everything for His glory. I have lied, cheated, disobeyed my parents aplenty, stolen things, and have been mean and unkind to family and friends. Maybe I haven't done anything to get me thrown in jail, but God has made it clear what His high standards are. I have done what God tells me not to do, and not done what God tells me is right. If you were a judge, Karen, would I be innocent or guilty of sin?"

"By that definition, you'd be guilty," Karen warily rendered the verdict.

"And God tells us in the Bible exactly what sinners deserve: eternal punishment for sin."

"But Elizabeth, you're not that bad. You're a good person. Surely you'll get into heaven," pleaded Karen.

"But Karen, you judged rightly yourself. I am guilty of sin. If you were a judge who had just sentenced a guilty criminal, and he began telling you what a nice guy he was and how he took care of his sick mother, would you just let him go?" asked Elizabeth.

"No," Karen answered.

"Think how much more a holy and righteous judge would uphold the guilty verdict for me. That's the bad news for me, Karen, and would you agree that it's bad news for you, too?" she asked sincerely of her friend.

"Yes, I think so," Karen admitted.

"Good!" exclaimed Elizabeth in a cheerful voice.

"What's so good about that? According to you, we're both doomed to hell!" exclaimed Karen in shock to match Elizabeth's exuberance.

"That's the bad news. Let's talk about the good news again. Remember how God sent His Son Jesus Christ to save people? Have you ever wondered what He saves people from? And what Jesus saves people for? We deserve hell, but Jesus can save and rescue us from that punishment that we admittedly deserve."

"Huh," grunted Karen thoughtfully.

Elizabeth continued, "Jesus died on the cross when He was without sin in order to pay the death price for any sinner who would believe in Him as their Lord and Savior."

"So that's how that works," said Karen more expressively.

Elizabeth decided to lay everything on the line. "Karen, I have put my trust in Jesus Christ to be my Lord and Savior. Have you?"

"When you explain things that way, I don't think I ever have. I just thought I was a good Christian girl because I showed up to church sometimes. Boy, that sounds really weak compared to the seriousness of my sin. I guess I'd better pray and ask Jesus to save me!" Karen bowed her head and silently prayed to God for a few minutes. When she looked up with bright eyes, she noticed that Elizabeth still had a serious look on her face. "What?"

"Karen, there's more."

"OK, let me have it," replied Karen.

"Don't misunderstand me, Karen. I am rejoicing with the angels in heaven that you have called out to God to save you. And God does promise to forgive all of your sins, past, present and future. But until we're glorified and perfected in heaven, we've got to do battle with our sins."

"And that brings us back to Pastor Eric's message this morning about the sin of gluttony, right?" Karen asked.

"That's right, Karen."

"Tell you what, Elizabeth. I don't think we should fast until I get this all straightened out. I'm hungry. Let's go grab some lunch – a light lunch – and go over what Pastor Eric was teaching about from the Bible this morning. Maybe we'll even join the follow-up counseling together."

Elizabeth walked with her friend back to the car. She was so amazed at how God had used this crisis to draw Karen closer to Him. Her own faith had been strengthened as she had reviewed these truths about salvation with Karen. And now, by God's grace, Elizabeth was ready to deal with her sinful eating habits in a way that would bring glory to God.

Chapter 10

Every morning the week after his sermon, Eric woke early to pray for his congregation and to ask for wisdom and compassion to deal with them in a humble and loving way. He would grab a few cards from the pile and pray for each person as he read their responses. Then he divided the cards into those who were repentant and interested in counseling, and those who were just angry and confused. He wanted to be prepared to respond to them personally in the upcoming days and weeks to come. His New Year's resolution was to speak the truth in love and especially work on how to love the people to whom he had spoken the hard truth.

When the church elders met again, Eric gave them a report about the responses to the sermon about gluttony.

"We have had a large response from our church members over the issue of gluttony, over 300 cards that I've read through this week. We heard a lot of angry responses when people left the building after the sermon, but very few angry comments were written. We should respond quickly to them, at least to those who signed their name. I've been thanking God that they took the opportunity to fill out a card. We can pray for them today, then assign someone to give them a call.

"Most of the responses, however, are from many beloved friends in our congregation who have humbly confessed their personal conviction over this issue, who desire to know what to do now and get some accountability with others. Now I don't want to start a big diet program at the church, but what can we, and should we, do to continue to teach and encourage the congregation?" Eric asked the elders.

Bill Sanderson, the elder who headed the Biblical counseling ministry at Grace Community Church, recommended some tools for personal evaluation, similar to the questions Eric had asked himself about his eating experience on Thanksgiving. He offered to tailor one of his general evaluation forms about mortifying sin to specifically address gluttony. Bill defined the old-fashioned term *mortifying sin* as seriously dealing with sin, from identifying and resisting temptation early to taking drastic measures to fight it off at every opportunity. Everyone wanted to learn more about it. The elders took note of the Bible passages Bill recommended for battling sin, knowing that they could counsel others with them as well as study them for personal application.

"The Biblical counseling department is not designed to be staffed by professionals who are the only qualified people to talk to members about life and sin," Bill explained. "Each counselor is trained to apply Scripture in their own lives first before counseling others. Then, our counselors guide and challenge fellow believers to apply God's Word in their own lives. This model is extended when a believer has experience applying God's Word before reaching out to others in a similar struggle. With such a great response in this case, we need to train up as many members as we can who are ready to apply God's Word to this issue, who will then be able to reach out to others around them for encouragement and accountability."

The elders agreed to consider putting together a series or course about mortifying the sin of gluttony, reaching out to others for encouragement and accountability, and learning new skills to create good habits for future victory with eating and exercise. With so many people involved, they wanted to open the church doors wide for training but also encourage people to open the doors of their homes to spend time with small groups or accountability partners.

In addition to the Biblical course of study, the elders saw a need for practical lessons regarding food and exercise. They would look for people within their congregation who already had knowledge or expertise to share. Rather than the church administrating a program and keeping records on individuals, the elders desired to connect members to partners who would hold each other accountable. Pastor Eric suggested a simple tracking sheet, with contact information on top, and space to note meetings, activities, phone calls, prayer requests, and even tracking weight.

Although at first they tried to avoid it, the elders began to recognize that one standard measurement would be a helpful tool for accountability: weight. It could be measured, easily monitored, and would reveal progress in eating less and exercising more. While it did not necessarily reveal the heart attitudes, it could certainly indicate changes in behavior.

Before the meeting closed, the door swung wide open and Stan Merriwether marched in.

"Well, gentlemen. I hope you're telling Pastor Eric how out-of-line his sermon was and insisting on his apology to this congregation," Stan puffed loudly.

"Good evening, Stan," Bill offered as a greeting. "We're wrapping up our elders meeting, but we would be happy to review the elders' position with you for a few minutes. Please take a seat." When space was cleared for him to join the group, he settled in his seat, expecting to get his satisfaction.

"Did you all read your Bibles this week? Did you find any example in there of the kind of attack Pastor Eric made on the large people of his congregation? I don't think so." Stan demanded.

"Actually, Stan, I did find an example in my Bible," said one of the younger elders, to the surprise of Stan and the others. "I found several examples of confrontations over various types of sin. The first one comes right after one man, who was extremely hungry after fasting for forty days, was tempted with food yet did not sin. In Matthew 4:17 we read: *'From that time Jesus began to preach and say, "Repent, for the kingdom of heaven is at hand."'* Jesus repeatedly preached repentance to crowds of sinful people in a very direct manner. But not just to embarrass or hurt them, or shock them into shaping up to try to be good enough. Jesus taught that when we take a good look at all the sinful stuff we do and think and say, then we more clearly see our need for a Savior. Then when Jesus saves us, we want to obey God and stop sinning."

Stan stood up quietly and marched back out the door.

"Do you guys want to hear the other examples I found?" the young elder asked expectantly.

The next week, Eric eagerly anticipated his meeting with Bill Sanderson to review the Biblical counseling materials Bill had modified to address the sin of gluttony. When Bill entered the office, Eric stood to greet him and was surprised because Bill was only carrying one sheet of paper tucked into his Bible.

"Glad you could come in today, Bill. Are you ready to talk about this can of worms I've opened?" Eric asked casually. "Or as I like to think of it, let's talk about the elephant in the room."

"Yes, Eric. I've been praying and working on this for several hours over the past week. I'm excited to see what the Lord is going to do in our congregation. But first, I was excited to see what the Lord wanted to show me about my own sinful habits," confessed Bill.

"You?" Eric asked in surprise. "You are a healthy, fit young man, Bill. Surely you don't have a problem with gluttony, do you?"

"When I look at my eating habits compared to Scripture, I have certainly sinned in this area. But I'm not surprised, Eric. Whenever I compare myself to God's holy standards, I know that I'm going to fall short. But I also know that I'm going to find a loving God who sent His perfect Son to be the propitiation for my sins."

"Amen to that!"

"I also know that I'm going to find some instruction and motivation for change, and it's not about the notches in my belt. I want to take every aspect of my life, compare it to Scripture, and make changes so that I will be pleasing to God. I am confident that I am saved, not based on my goodness at all. But I love God so much that

I want to follow Him and please Him as much as I can while I'm on earth. That will bring a blessing on my life and my family, and make me a more effective evangelist," concluded Bill.

"Wow! Thanks for your perspective, Bill," enthused Eric. "It has been a serious matter of prayer about whether to bring this issue to the congregation. But if our motivation is to please the Lord with our lives, then we will welcome this challenge. After all, God does give us the instruction and motivation to do it, and that's after He completely covers our sin with forgiveness.

"So what have you got for me today?" asked Eric, ready to tackle this issue from the right perspective.

"This is not an easy sin to deal with," Bill began, "but God's Word shows us a simple plan of attack to mortify sin. It's based on several passages in the New Testament that call believers to put off sinful habits and put on righteousness. Here's one of those verses," Bill said as he opened his Bible. "Ephesians 4:22-24 says, *'that, in reference to your former manner of life, you lay aside the old self, which is being corrupted in accordance with the lusts of deceit, and that you be renewed in the spirit of your mind, and put on the new self, which in the likeness of God has been created in righteousness and holiness of the truth.'*

"But mortifying sin starts with confession. When we call sin sin, then believers can humbly confess and repent to begin to deal with their problems. One of the hardest things is to get started in the right way, correctly identifying the root of the problem. The world likes to give labels to problems, but they usually blame someone or something else. That takes away the power to make any changes. But when we correctly identify that our problems are rooted in our own sin, then we have hope to make changes. And God wants to empower believers to become more like Christ. After all, that's one of the main reasons He sent the Holy Spirit, to use His Word in our hearts for sanctification, right?

"So let's look at how we can do that," Bill continued. "This worksheet has only eight questions, but the plan is to work through correctly identifying the sin, confessing it, putting it off and figuring out what thoughts, words, and actions to put on instead. This final step of putting on righteousness is essential. God's Word is unique in its wisdom regarding this. I am reminded of the story that Jesus told in Matthew 12 about a man trying to morally reform. The unclean spirit left. His heart was swept and put in order but remained unoccupied. So, the unclean spirit came back and brought his friends, making things worse than before. In our situation, by the power of God we need to put off sin in the first place, but if we don't go that additional step in His power to put on righteousness by creating new thoughts and habits, then our sin can easily come back. We know this truth from Scripture, but we also need God's power to apply it."

"OK, let's take a look at what you've got," said Eric as they turned their eyes to that single sheet of paper. Here were the eight personal evaluation questions listed on that sheet.

1. What exactly happened and what did I do? (Write out the detailed circumstances and actions.)

2. What was I thinking? Or what are my thoughts about it now?

3. Circle my actions that were sinful. Write the Bible word for that sin here. Circle my thoughts that were sinful. Write the Bible word for that sin here.

4. The sinful actions and thoughts listed in #3 should be put off; stop doing them. What right things should I put on instead? List them here with a Scripture reference to support it. (Write out the full verse on the back side of this paper.)

5. Seek forgiveness from God and others, if necessary. What else do I need to do to fix the current problem (share, return or replace something)?

6. When I am tempted by this sin in the future, what should I pray or think? Write out your prayer and memorize a supporting Scripture verse. Include a specific request for God's wisdom, strength to stop sinful actions and do the right thing, and forgiveness.

7. When I am tempted by this sin in the future, what will I do to implement my right thoughts? "Out of the overflow of the heart the mouth speaks" (Matthew 12:34b). Write out words to say and any actions (such as saying *No* out loud or leaving a location with temptations).

8. Thank God for any small or large victories! Return to God for forgiveness and wisdom and strength! Get in the habit of practicing godliness when not in the midst of a trial.

Eric recognized some of the steps he had taken several weeks ago when he was considering his own sinful habits. He had worked through the confession and repenting parts, but he had not gone far enough into putting them off and putting on new thoughts and habits. He was looking forward to completing his personal examination now that he knew the next few steps of the process.

"Thank you, Bill, for putting this together. I see what I need to do in my own heart examination. Would you be willing to meet with me in a few days to talk about my own issues? I want to make sure I'm on the right track since I'll be leading a lot more people in this process. Are you available to take a role in this, too?"

"Yes, Eric, as your brother in Christ, I would consider it a privilege to exhort and encourage you in this process. What do you have in mind for the rest of the congregation? I have a few trained Biblical counselors, but we can't properly minister to every member at the same time."

"You're right. It's too big a group for our counselors to deal with each person. No, the elders are in agreement that we need to train our congregation to examine themselves first before ministering to one another. Having this worksheet to start with will help, so perhaps you can meet with the group as a whole to explain how it works and give examples."

"Sounds like a good plan. Shall we set some dates? Next week, you and me. In a few weeks, the whole gang!" said Bill enthusiastically.

Chapter 11

Eric had spent several hours searching through and studying the Bible when he had prepared for his first sermon on gluttony, plus many more hours examining his personal life habits regarding the sin of gluttony. One of the passages he studied had given Eric an idea for a basic structure for an accountability program. When they had a quiet evening at home, he shared his ideas with Jennifer. Eric opened his Bible.

"Listen to this passage of Scripture that I have been thinking about. It's Colossians 1:9-12. *'For this reason also, since the day we heard of it, we have not ceased to pray for you and to ask that you may be filled with the knowledge of His will in all spiritual wisdom and understanding, so that you will walk in a manner worthy of the Lord, to please Him in all respects, bearing fruit in every good work and increasing in the knowledge of God, strengthened with all power, according to His glorious might, for the attaining of all steadfastness and patience, joyously giving thanks to the Father, who has qualified us to share in the inheritance of the saints in light.'"*

"That's a great passage, Eric, full of wisdom and encouragement for the Christian life. I've read it and used it when I've been praying for friends, or needing a word or phrase to send in notes of encouragement," said Jennifer. "What were you thinking about?"

On their home office whiteboard, Eric started to make a list of ten points from the Colossians passage that he thought might serve as an outline to a simple accountability program between two church members. The points he wrote were:

1) praying for each other
2) studying God's Word to be filled with wisdom and understanding
3) walking
4) pleasing God
5) a fruit activity
6) good works, such as a service project
7) studying God's Word some more
8) strength training exercises
9) practicing steadfastness and patience, and
10) joyously giving thanks.

As Jennifer looked again at the Bible verses, she could see how Eric had extracted these points.

"I'm not really trying to create a new diet and exercise program," Eric explained to his wife, "but I'm looking for some kind of framework to give to our congregation as we all start talking to each other about these issues and holding one another accountable to put off sinful behavior and put on some new habits."

"Ten weeks is a reasonable length of time to commit to an activity," said Jennifer realistically. "I think you would need to explain your overall plan and clarify some of your points more. I'm relieved that you didn't try to make a 10-point alliteration!" she teased. "Some of the activities, like praying for one another, could be developed between the two people involved. It might be motivating for people to know they can share how they tried to apply this verse to their own situation and what they learned from it."

"I was talking to Wayne Long. Ever since the accident, he and his wife have been attending our church regularly. He was there for my sermon about gluttony and has been talking to me about how God's Word can be practically applied. As a sports coach and fitness expert who loves the Lord, he is willing to commit to lead a basic exercise class for ten Saturdays, although he will probably get interrupted somewhere in the middle when their baby is born," Eric chuckled.

"That will be helpful for a lot of people, I'm sure. And exercise seems to be the focus of number 3, walking, and number 8, strength training exercises. I know that I can walk," joked Jennifer, "but I'd like to learn about strength training. There are plenty of items on your list that involve Bible study, and that's your specialty, dear. But what's this number 5 about a fruit activity?" Jennifer asked warily.

"I have a few ideas about that. One idea I have for good works would be to serve at the Harvest Hope Food Bank. I thought maybe our family could go check it out this weekend. Are you and the kids available?" Eric asked.

"Let's put it on the schedule," said Jennifer, pleased with that idea.

Saturday dawned cool and rainy. It would have been a good day to stay inside and watch a game on TV. Instead, this was the day Eric and his family were going to volunteer at Harvest Hope Food Bank of Georgia, inside the warehouse at least. A few other families from his church congregation had contacted the food bank to help today, too. The Harvey family climbed into the car, headed west and arrived a few minutes before 9:00. They entered a large, clean warehouse half-filled with shelves of giant boxes on pallets stacked to the ceiling. Another area was clear and organized for volunteers to work at tables, with piles of smaller cardboard boxes ready to be assembled and filled. In such a big space, it wasn't surprising that it was a little cool. Good thing they wore sweatshirts.

"Thank you all for coming," the coordinator greeted the small crowd. "Today you will be helping us in product recovery. Several retail stores in South Georgia are generous to send us products from their stores, either overstock, near to expiration, or slightly damaged merchandise. Also, regional farms donate food in bulk. We can turn these valuable items into substantial meals for needy families in our community. But we need your help to sort through these huge bins to put together 20-pound food boxes that can supplement meals for a family of four for about one week. Today, we're looking for main staples: grains such as rice or pasta, beans or canned meat, and fruits and vegetables. We will collect any sugary treats and add them later when appropriate, but we want to focus on nutrition today. We will have some smaller bins to collect other goodies you might find such as cosmetics, diapers, and office or cleaning supplies. If you have any questions, please ask. Now, if you will gather yourselves into groups of about six people, we'll get you to a work table."

"Is it OK, Dad, if I work with Rachel and her parents for a while?" Hannah asked.

"And can Jeremy and Rick work with us?" Samuel asked right after his sister.

"I guess that will be all right," replied Eric as he looked at Jennifer.

"Let's have a contest, Hannah, and see who can empty the first bin," challenged Samuel.

"Or maybe who can complete the most food boxes," Hannah suggested, getting into the spirit.

For nearly two hours they worked with their hands to dig through the bins. After tidying up their work tables and sweeping the debris scattered on the floor, the volunteers gathered together again at the front of the warehouse to hear the coordinator's final announcement.

"Wow, what a great bunch of hard workers you were today! You sorted through twenty large bins and put together over 100 food boxes that will be distributed to some needy families in our community. Good job, everyone!" Everyone joined in the cheer. Samuel gave Hannah a thumbs-up.

"So Dad, Jeremy, Rick and I were calculating. If those boxes help to feed a family of four for one week, that's about 80 individual meals. For all the boxes we did today, that would be 800 meals," explained Samuel proudly.

"Check your math, buddy. One hundred boxes multiplied by 80 would be 8,000 meals," Eric explained.

"Guys, did you hear that?" Samuel ran back to talk to his friends.

Hannah put her arm around her dad. "I'm worn out, but I'm sure glad we came to serve today."

"Me, too, Hannah. Me, too," sighed Eric. This experience turned out to be another helpful perspective on food for Eric's consideration, both in his personal life and in his plans for an accountability program for his congregation.

The family meal at the Harveys on the appointed Sunday afternoon was a great opportunity for Wayne Long and his wife Cindy to get to know Pastor Eric personally as well as make friends with Chris and Ashley Harvey, who had been married for a few years just like the Longs.

"Welcome," Eric greeted his guests. He had changed out of his suit from Sunday morning services and had a large apron covering his jeans and a button-down shirt. "My wife made some great salads, but I'm in charge of the barbecue. Our meals on Sunday aren't at regular meal times. Go ahead and grab a plate of snacks and a drink and make yourselves comfortable in the backyard while I work on this meat."

Eric introduced Wayne and Cindy to his wife Jennifer and their two younger children, then left them in the care of Chris and Ashley. These two younger couples had some things in common as they talked about outdoor adventures and favorite restaurants. One difference was that Cindy was obviously seven months pregnant. After some general conversation, the guys paired off, and the young ladies settled into a friendly conversation.

"So you must be excited about becoming a parent," Ashley said encouragingly, opening up a fun conversation.

"Oh, yes. It's something Wayne and I have waited for for years. Whenever he would go to Afghanistan, part of me would hope I was pregnant before he left, and part of me was relieved when I wasn't so I wouldn't have to worry about parenting alone. Now that Wayne is working locally with a normal Monday through Friday job, I'm just so thankful to know he'll be around for me during the pregnancy and for our baby," Cindy admitted candidly.

Cindy was not too tall, and her figure was naturally soft but was even fuller with her pleasantly protruding belly. Her straight dark hair was cut to shoulder length and fell in a flattering frame around her face. There was a pleasant blend of nationalities to her coloring, but her major features were clearly Asian-influenced.

"So is Pastor Eric your dad or your husband's dad?" Cindy asked.

Ashley laughed politely and explained, "Eric is Chris' dad. But everyone tells us that we could pass for brother and sister since we have similar coloring and features. We've been together for a long time, since high school, and I've grown up a lot in this house. Jennifer has been the ideal mother-in-law. She was discipling me way back in high school before I really knew Chris. She has continued to be such a good influence on me." Ashley smiled at the older woman coming towards them.

"Hi, girls. Are you enjoying this beautiful weather? Cindy, I'm so glad you could join us today. Are you comfortable? Do you need anything?" Jennifer asked.

"I'm just fine. Thanks for inviting us over. It's good for Wayne and me to get to know some people in the church better. We need some Christian friends outside of the military," Cindy explained a bit shyly.

Ashley offered to include Cindy in some of the church activities she was involved with. "And I'm happy to show you around town, too."

"That would be great. Wayne has been taking me over to the medical center on the Marine Base for my checkups, but his schedule is busy with the Marine recruiting and coaching at the Youth Clubs right now. With his truck in the shop for repairs, he can still jog or ride his bike to work. But maybe you could give me a ride to an appointment later this week?" Cindy asked.

"Sure, just let me know when and where. I've never really been to the base, even though it's not far from town. It will be fun to check it out with you before or after your appointment."

Cindy and Ashley could tell that they had started a new friendship that day.

Chapter 12

After a few weeks, when Pastor Eric and the elders felt that they had developed a reasonable plan with helpful handouts and expert instruction, they invited the congregation to an introductory meeting. Most members who had responded positively to Eric's sermon signed up right away. Several who had reacted with anger to his message had been personally contacted by Biblical counselors from church or encouraged by friends to prayerfully reconsider. Others were simply curious and showed up to the meeting.

"Oh, Lord, thank You for what You have been doing in my heart and how Your Word has changed my life. I pray for the people gathering tonight, that they would be motivated by their love for You to put off sin and put on righteousness. More than that, Lord, I thank You for the body of Christ, the church, a community of believers that You have brought together to serve one another and help one another. I confess, Lord, that I have not fully examined my own sinful food choices, but that I am in the same sanctifying process as others. Use me to point them to Christ and to Your Word of truth. You have changed me. I believe You can change them, too. Bless this night, Lord, for Your glory and our good. Amen."

"Thank you all for coming to talk about the elephant in the room," greeted Eric after the crowd of over one hundred had settled into the seats of the church sanctuary. "I realize that many of you have never talked to anyone about gluttony before. The first Sunday of this year was the first time I had ever preached about it, and I don't know if

I've ever heard another sermon addressing it. Since most of you are here because you heard my whole sermon, let me quickly summarize what I discovered in the Bible about gluttony. Then, I want to share with you how the Lord has been working in our congregation recently, first to bring you all here today, and then to raise up individuals from our congregation to guide and motivate us as we start to mortify the sin of gluttony and look for ways to put on righteousness. Just to clarify for everyone: we are using the term *mortifying sin*, which means to deal drastically with our sins by fighting every temptation. But we all need to know what to look out for and what spiritual weapons to use in this battle, so God has graciously and clearly provided that information in His Word, the Bible. Later I will invite some members to come up and introduce some things we've put together to help you not only examine your own sin but to facilitate open communication of exhortation and encouragement as we walk through this together as a church family. By the end of the night, I hope you will have several options for how to get started on this journey with the Bible as your guide."

Eric got right to the point. "Gluttony is the sinful over-consumption of food, or drink, for the wrong reasons. When we eat too much, it is a sin because we're greedy and not good stewards of the abundance God has provided for our use. When we eat for another purpose besides fueling our bodies, it usually encompasses the sins of idolizing ourselves or looking for satisfaction from the wrong thing. When we eat in a way that does not glorify God, we sin by breaking the first commandment.

"We will look at some of the natural consequences of gluttony along the way, but we won't make them our main focus. We know that they range from upset stomachs and missed opportunities to obesity and its related illnesses. In our attempt to make goals and check progress, we will have to use some practical measuring and monitoring device, and that will be a weight scale." Some in the audience cringed.

Eric continued, "While our church does not want to start a diet program, we do want to help our members to apply God's Word to every aspect of our lives. Since this challenge has been accepted by such a large group, we have been working on plans to first help you to examine and address your own areas of sin, and then we want to encourage you who become more mature believers to reach out to others in our congregation who are battling sin. This is Biblical counseling and Christian fellowship at its best.

"Let me present to you our theme Bible passage, Colossians 1:9-12: *'For this reason also, since the day we heard of it, we have not ceased to pray for you and to ask that you may be filled with the knowledge of His will in all spiritual wisdom and understanding, so that you will walk in a manner worthy of the Lord, to please Him in all respects, bearing fruit in every good work and increasing in the knowledge of God, strengthened with all power, according to His glorious might, for the attaining of all steadfastness and patience, joyously giving thanks to the Father, who has qualified us to share in the inheritance of the saints in light.'*

"From this verse, we have created a basic ten-week accountability program. On this first handout, you will see the ten themes for each week starting in February. You will see prayer and Bible study, exercise and projects. We wanted to give you a variety of ways to address your personal issues as well as give you a platform for reaching out to others.

"Next, I would like to introduce to you our elder over Biblical counseling, Bill Sanderson. Thanks for coming today, Bill. Please teach us what you have learned," said Eric to segue the meeting into the fine details of personal examination.

Bill distributed the handouts of a Biblical counseling journaling page based on the series of eight questions for mortifying sin that he had discussed with Eric. Also, he had created an example page, admitting that he had examined one of his recent eating experiences. The crowd was surprised that this elder would be so transparent to admit his own struggles, but they were also greatly encouraged as he went on to explain the hope of change after applying God's Word to the situation.

"Thanks, Bill," said Eric as they made a transition to a new topic. "Now I would like to introduce you to an enthusiastic young man in our congregation, Wayne Long. Now don't be intimidated by his bulging muscles or military haircut. He's really a nice guy. Some of your kids might know him as the coach for the Youth Clubs. He and his wife Cindy have been attending our church faithfully ever since my father-in-law Leonard ran into him on Thanksgiving." People who knew about the accident chuckled. "He's here to help and teach us. Tell us what you're going to do, Wayne," said Eric before he stepped to the side.

"I'm thankful to God for using me in His church," Wayne began humbly. "I never imagined that the fitness training I got at home, in the Marines, and in college could be used by God in this way. I have offered to teach a free exercise class for ten weeks on Saturday mornings. It will be focused on helping beginners create a work-out routine that is reasonable for their condition and setting realistic goals so that they will actually do their workout. So, come out and give it a try!"

"So, we have three new tools to help us start drastically dealing with the sin of gluttony: a ten-week accountability plan, a Biblical counseling journaling page for self-examination, and a free exercise program." Before Eric could say any more, the crowd began to ap-plaud. They were excited and thankful.

"As we close, I want to challenge you to commit to a couple of goals. When I was researching New Year's resolutions, people suc-ceeded when they had set specific and measurable goals. Here are the two goals that I would like you all to consider making: First, make a commitment to lose 20 pounds in the next ten weeks by eating less and exercising more. That's averaging two pounds per week. I'm not going to give you specifics; I want you to discover what works for you, but the plan is to decrease your intake by eating less food and increase your output by burning more calories through action. At our weekly exercise class with Wayne Long, we will have a scale available for you to weigh yourself and make a note. If you weigh yourself at home, then I encourage you to only do so once per week to keep the right perspective on it. After all, our ultimate goal is not a certain number but to put off the sin of gluttony and put on righteousness to be pleasing to God.

"The second specific and measurable goal is to talk to your accountability partner at least once per week. It's easy to check your calendar to see if you did it or not. Once again, I'm trusting the Lord that these conversations will be edifying to each of you in your pursuit of holiness. It should be iron sharpening iron as it says in Proverbs 27:17."

As he ended the meeting, Eric referred the people to the table where Jennifer was distributing information about accountability partners. Those who had registered for this meeting on-line had been given the opportunity to sign up for a partner to be assigned tonight. Others could sign up now and wait to be paired up.

The sanctuary volume increased as people began to meet and greet one another. Elizabeth and her friend Karen, who had asked to be accountability partners, talked excitedly about the materials they had received. Sarah was pleased to meet an older woman who could disciple her, but she looked around for Giselle, hoping she would show up and get help, too. Beverly Douglas was paired with the young woman, Stephany, who had been attending their church for the past couple of years. Leonard Douglas was over talking to Wayne Long. Pastor Eric wondered if they would be paired together because Eric did not realize that Wayne had signed up to participate. Eric thought that it was ironic that as accountability partners, these two men's lives would become intertwined, just like their vehicles had been on the night of the accident. But Eric recognized that they would, in fact, make a good pair since they shared a military background. Many other people were pairing up and talking enthusiastically. Eric stood back and smiled as he watched the congregation.

"Hi, Pastor Eric. It looks like we'll be accountability partners," said the jolly man in the red shirt, Nick Saint.

"Mrs. Douglas?" asked the young lady as she approached Beverly.

"Yes, that's me. But please call me Beverly. You must be Stephany Goodacre. I'm so glad to meet you. I think I've seen you around church, but we must not be in the same fellowship group," Beverly said as she tried to be welcoming and friendly in what could be an awkward situation, two large ladies getting together to talk about gluttony.

"I've been attending Grace Church for a few years now, but I don't often get to a fellowship group. I have shared custody of my children so our weekend schedules can be a little irregular," Stephany admitted. She appeared to be in her early 40s with beautiful ebony skin and an afro that framed her face as she pulled it back with a wide, brightly colored headband. Her physical build was very similar to Beverly's. About 5 feet 6 inches tall, they both had too much weight for their average frames. Another feature that they both shared was a bright and friendly smile. That was probably what Jennifer thought of when she matched these two women together.

"Let's double-check the contact information they gave us so that we can stay in touch. Then let's take a few minutes today to share some prayer requests, since Pastor Eric's schedule starts with praying for one another," Beverly prompted. "I would be delighted to pray for you regarding any praise or need, but we'll have to start talking about our particular challenges related to food, too. Let's start with the easy stuff. What are you thankful for this week, Stephany?"

Stephany was a little taken-aback. "You know, it's been such a tough week that I haven't stopped to think about any good things. I got my paycheck on Friday and was able to get groceries before my weekend with the kids. My ex-husband took them to a school event today which left me free to come here for the meeting. Those are blessings, aren't they?"

"Yes, they sure are," said Beverly with a warm smile. "I always look at my family to start counting my blessings. Is there a particular need or request that I can be praying for?"

"Well, I don't want to sit here complaining and gossiping about my ex-husband, but I sure need God's wisdom to deal with him." It was clear that Stephany was upset about something, but also pretty sad, too.

"Thank you for your restraint in how you speak about him. I don't need to know the details to be able to pray for you. But God already knows the details, so He's the right one to bring our cares and concerns to, right? Now, here comes the hard part, Stephany, telling each other how we can be praying for each other regarding the sin of gluttony. I don't think we can delve deeply into it now, but I hope that we can build a relationship of trust, accountability, and encouragement as we spend time together over the next few weeks. Would you agree that we both struggle with gluttony?" They eyed each other for a moment, then began nodding their heads with sheepish grins. "And do we both acknowledge that there must be sin that we've been harboring in this area?"

"I don't really understand that part yet," admitted Stephany.

"It's a new way of thinking about it for me, too, dear. I'm excited that the church elders have given us some tools to start thinking about it that way, and as we study our Bibles I think God will help us to understand, don't you?" asked Beverly.

"Yes, I guess so," said Stephany, but she didn't seem too sure.

"Well, let's stop and pray for a few minutes right now. Then we'll check our schedules. Are you available to come with me for a pedicure this week? That's one of my favorite things. And it's my treat!"

Chapter 13

A few days after the meeting at church, Wayne Long dropped by Leonard Douglas's house. Leonard was finishing up some yard work. It was another pleasant day in between rain storms, so Leonard was removing soggy leaves from his rain gutters. He was ready for a break, so he invited Wayne to join him in his den for some lemonade.

"Wow, sir," Wayne commented as he looked around the den which was decorated with memorabilia and awards from Leonard's military career. "This is quite a collection from a distinguished career. Vietnam, huh?"

"Yep. Those were some tough years, but I was glad to serve my country and glad to get out alive. Tell me about your years of service, young man." After talking about Wayne's more recent and shorter military career, they moved on to other topics. Wayne assured Leonard that his truck was back to normal after the accident.

"It's been great for my wife and me to get plugged in at Grace Church. Since moving into town and away from the military base, we have been looking for a church with expository Bible teaching and true Christian fellowship, and we definitely found what we were looking for," said Wayne. "I enjoy volunteering for the sports and fitness programs at the Youth Clubs of Albany right now, and Pastor Eric's accountability program will be a good challenge for me, too."

"I had a good career with the Marines, Wayne, but I'm thankful for the civilian life with my wife. She was a trooper, following me to assignments around the country, and waiting faithfully for my re-turn during a few tough deployments." Leonard looked back down the hall to the kitchen where he knew Beverly was keeping up a lovely home for him. "Being trapped in the accident reminded me how precious my wife is to me. It also challenged us to confront our sinful habits and their dangerous consequences, which led us to talk to Eric about our gluttony. We appreciate you helping out with the exercise program. You don't seem to have a problem with overeat-ing, so why did you sign up for the accountability program?"

"Well, sir, I have lived a pretty disciplined life as a son of a Ma-rine drill sergeant and a Marine in my own right. I don't think I've had to battle the sin of gluttony, but I've had my share of sin to deal with. God is holy, and He calls His followers to holy living. That's the standard I strive for, but I know that I cannot do it on my own strength or will. I'm willing to examine myself about how I make food choices if that's an area that God wants to work on in me. But I think the mortifying sin worksheet and accountability with other believers is a model for any area of sin we need to work on." Wayne continued. "It seems to me that Eric had it right. If we call sin sin, then we can deal with it the way God wants us to according to the Bible. Repent. Put off. Put on."

Easier said than done, Leonard thought to himself.

"It's been great getting to know Pastor Eric, your family and the members of Grace Church over the past few months. I'm excited about putting together an exercise program for the people in the church," Wayne said, trying to get some feedback from Leonard.

"Most of us aren't tough enough for a Marine workout, son," Leonard laughed as he patted his substantial belly.

Wayne laughed too. "Most Marines don't start out tough enough for a Marine workout either. No, we've got to start with the basics. I want to introduce people to a variety of ways to exercise so that they have a wide range of choices to find things that they will actually do. That's the hardest part about exercise, getting started and continu-ing to do it. Nike sure got their slogan right. Just do it."

Changing to a more serious but gentle tone, Wayne bravely asked, "Sir, if you don't mind my asking, now that we're accountability partners, can you tell me what's your battle?" Wayne indicated that he wasn't laughing at Leonard's waistline.

"You know, I've been asking myself those questions for a few weeks. After the accident," Leonard looked at Wayne in a significant way, "Beverly and I were more hurt about something we heard rather than our physical injuries. The firemen had to saw through our car frame to rescue us because we were too fat to pull out. As we were recovering at home, Beverly and I admitted that we needed to do something about this embarrassing problem, but we also admitted that we had never been serious about battling it before. We needed to take a different approach, a spiritual approach, and see what God had to say about it. So, we talked to Eric and started our Bible study.

"I'm working through those questions that Eric gave us about examining our eating habits. I know that I enjoy generous portions at meal time but don't do enough activity in my retirement. But there's something else." Leonard hesitated. Did he want to confess his problem to this young kid? On the other hand, maybe another Marine would understand what Leonard was going through. "I don't want to worry my wife about it, but since I retired about ten years ago, I have lots of trouble sleeping."

"Nightmares?" Wayne asked gently. "The war?"

"Yep. And when I can't sleep, I get up and eat."

"And you think your wife doesn't know?" Wayne asked doubtfully.

"I don't want to worry her," said Leonard.

"You don't think she notices the missing food?" Wayne asked doubtfully again.

"Well, between the two of us, we go through a lot of groceries," Leonard tried to joke, but he was kind of sad about it.

"Pastor Eric said that gluttony involved eating food for the wrong reasons. Do you think you are eating at night trying to find comfort from your nightmares?"

"That's the conclusion I've come to, Wayne."

"Well, sir, how's that been working for you? Have you found comfort?" Wayne asked respectfully.

"Not really. I'm fat and unhealthy and still have those nightmares," Leonard admitted.

"That's because food is for the body, not the soul. God offers comfort for our soul through salvation in Jesus Christ and the indwelling Comforter of the Holy Spirit. And the Holy Spirit works in us through Scripture, not food. Did you know that the Bible says 'do not fear' 365 times? That's one for every day of the year!" Wayne explained.

"Hey, that might be a good project for me in the middle of the night, to find all of those verses, one a day until I find them all!" Leonard replied with much more hope. Leonard was actually relieved that he had shared his troubles with this young man. He even asked Wayne to hold him accountable to complete that project. "And maybe I'll join your exercise program," Leonard said sheepishly.

"Clothe yourselves with humility," Beverly read from 1 Peter 5:5. Since Beverly had been a large woman for decades, she had created a fashionable style by maintaining an extensive wardrobe. While she knew that battling the sin of gluttony did not require her to dress like a dowdy monk, she was considering how to focus on clothing herself with humility.

"What do you think this means, Jennifer?" Beverly asked her daughter about 1 Peter 5:5 one afternoon while she was visiting.

"Well, humility in the Bible refers to recognizing your true position as a sinful creature before a holy and mighty God. I remember your verse in 1 Peter goes on to say, 'with humility toward one another,' so it's about our attitude towards ourselves and other people. I must remember that I am not more important than other people, then act like that's true."

"When I think of the word *clothe*, I think of the activity of getting dressed, including the preparations and the mirror check. So, if I clothe myself in humility, I need to spend some time every morning preparing my heart before going out among people," Beverly figured. "I need to think rightly about myself, a sinner saved by the grace of God that He can use to serve other people. Using Eric's model of putting off and putting on, I need to put off my pride and selfishness, and put on service to others."

"That's right, Mom," said Jennifer encouragingly. "Don't forget about God's warning and promise in the next verse. It says that God is opposed to the proud but gives grace to the humble."

"Wow!" exclaimed Beverly. "That's a great motivation. I don't want to be opposed by God. I need all of God's grace that I can get! Maybe I'll write these verses on my wardrobe mirror and read them every morning."

Chapter 14

A small crowd gathered in the all-purpose room at the reasonable hour of 9:00 a.m. on the first Saturday in February. Members of the congregation of all ages and sizes milled about, some in fancy athletic apparel but most in casual sweat pants. Everyone was subdued, looking around in slight embarrassment but also curious to see who had accepted the invitation. Some people found friends they weren't expecting to see. Sarah joined Elizabeth and Karen, who had arrived together. Before long, Wayne Long hopped up on the stage and called everyone to gather around him.

"Good morning, folks. Glad you could come out to the first of ten exercise classes for our church. I think it would be appropriate to open with a word of prayer. Pastor Eric?" Wayne looked over at Eric in his sweat pants while the eyes of the congregation opened a little wider to see their pastor there to exercise. After his brief prayer, everyone looked back at Wayne for instructions.

"My name is Wayne Long. I'm your friendly neighborhood Marine recruiter, and I have recently moved to Albany with my wife Cindy and joined the church. My dad was a drill sergeant, so I've been seriously exercising my whole life." The crowd laughed a little. "There's no way I can do a complete fitness evaluation for each one of you today. If you have concerns, you should definitely check with your doctor before starting any program. I'm planning to teach you a variety of basic fitness activities that you can use in your personal exercise routine. I have to warn you, though, I might miss a class when my wife has our baby sometime in March." The crowd cheered at the good news.

"My goal today is to get you started on your own exercise habits. Before I explain further, would you please spread out to make yourselves some personal space? After you slide out toward the side of the room, just stretch your arms out to your sides, then in front and back to make sure you don't hit anybody. Don't move too far away, though. I want you to be able to hear me without me using my drill sergeant voice."

Everyone complied quickly and quietly. "While I keep talking to finish my introduction, I would like each of you to gently march in place. No high knees or stomping necessary, this isn't the military, but let's start moving our bodies to get our blood pumping and bodies warmed up. Left, right, left, right. That's it. Nothing fancy." Wayne gave everyone a minute to get moving to the gentle pace.

"I'm ambitious. I want you to learn two things this morning. When I coach kids at the Youth Clubs, I hope they'll take home just one new thing at a time. But I think you can learn two things this morning. The first one is that walking is a great exercise, no matter what condition you are in. I realize that walking is number three on Pastor Eric's accountability program, but it is a great place to start your fitness program. With walking, you can keep it simple or rev it up to high gear. It is easy to monitor your own level and progress and make adjustments quickly. You can get a complete fitness experience from a good walk. Walking is a great exercise!

"The second thing I want you to learn is the basic pattern for a good fitness routine. There are four steps: warm-up, challenge, cool down, and stretching. I won't debate with you now about the myth about stretching first. I'll just challenge you to go home tonight and put a rubber band in the freezer. Tomorrow night, give it a pull and see what happens." Some in the crowd laughed because they could imagine what would happen to a frozen rubber band when stretched. Everyone understood the point that Wayne was trying to make about warming up before stretching.

"We're already warming up, just walking in place. Like the name says, you should feel your body getting warmer on the inside. The blood is pumping faster to every part of your body, and this should feel good. You shouldn't be straining or aching, although a few tight muscles should start to relax. You can get fancier in your warm-up routine, but this will work fine for our group this morning since I can keep talking for a few minutes before our challenge.

"The second step in a fitness routine is the challenge. Don't be afraid of the word *challenge*. Let me tell you the challenge for today. We are going to walk around the block of the church. Praise the Lord for such a beautiful day in February. For some of you, you have never walked around this block, so it will be a new experience. Be sure to look around. Enjoy the day. Guys, buddy up to fellowship with a brother in Christ. Ladies, this would be a great opportunity to start building a relationship with your accountability partner if she's here. If not, I see many friendly faces. Please, please, please, no cell phones or iPods; disconnect to connect. For your personal challenge, maybe you'll go around once, twice, or maybe you'll even lap your grandparents before you're ready to stop," Wayne said, looking at Samuel, who was standing between Beverly and Leonard.

"It's like we're marching around Jericho!" joked Samuel. Everyone who was familiar with the Bible story about the Israelites marching around Jericho before God made the walls come crashing down laughed at his observation.

"When you are done with your challenge, please come back into this room, but don't sit down unless you are feeling sick. Take a few minutes to cool down by moving around more slowly until your breathing is normal. Don't neglect this third step in your routine, the cool down."

"How do we know when we're back to normal?" Elizabeth asked from the crowd.

"One easy way to tell if you are back to normal is if you can carry on a normal conversation," Wayne replied.

"OK, Karen, you will like that test," Elizabeth teased.

"I'll be back in here after fifteen minutes of the challenge. For some of you, you will want to cool down at that point. Then I'll show you some basic stretches. After the cool down is the best time for the fourth step in your fitness routine, the stretching. For those who want to walk longer, keep walking around the block. I'll lead another session of stretches after thirty minutes. Does that make sense?"

Everyone nodded

"So, have you learned two things? Let's see. Who remembers the first thing I wanted to teach you?"

"Walking is great exercise," was heard from several points in the room.

"Good. This time, we'll play school. Raise your hand if you can tell me the four steps of a good fitness routine," said Wayne. While several hands were raised, Wayne called on Samuel.

"Warm up, challenge, cool down and stretch," said Samuel as he ticked them off on his fingers. His grandpa patted him on the back.

"Good job. I hope you all have learned these two things. Can you handle one more thing? I think you can," encouraged Wayne. "I want you to learn a Bible verse. When you engage your mind while you are exercising, you increase the benefits of the time spent. So, here's a great verse to think about, talk about on your walk, and try to memorize before you cool down. Galatians 5:25 says, *'If we live by the Spirit, let us also walk by the Spirit.'*"

"*'If we live by the Spirit, let us also walk by the Spirit.'*" Many people repeated the verse to begin learning it.

"Guess what? I've talked so long that you are all warmed up. It's time for the challenge. Let's go walk around the block because walking is good exercise! Have a great time, and I'll see you back in here for the cool down and stretch. Let's go!" And off went the crowd, walking, chatting, and chanting the Bible verse.

Later that afternoon, Jennifer noticed Hannah hanging out in her room, so she tapped lightly on the door.

"Hi, Mom. Come on in. Did you need something?" Hannah said pleasantly.

Sometimes teenagers could be moody, but Jennifer was thankful that the line of communication stayed open with Hannah. These were important years for kids as they morphed from children to adults. They wanted more freedom and responsibility, but they needed more wisdom and self-control.

"I was hoping this would be a good time to chat. Do you have a couple minutes for your mom?" Jennifer asked in a lighthearted way.

"Sure. What's on your mind?" Hannah responded as she closed her magazine and pulled the earbuds out from the sides of her head.

"You listened to your Dad's sermon last month about gluttony. And you've seen some of the good and angry responses to the challenge. You've also seen lots of activity around here as your dad and I figure out how to minister to those who have taken up the challenge to deal with this sin. Did you have fun at the exercise class today?" Hannah nodded to all of this while her mom continued. "I think you understood the points that Dad made in his sermon. But I wanted to talk to you about some of the issues and perspectives you might have as a young person getting bombarded by body images from the world, from TV, the Internet and magazines"—she gestured at Hannah's reading material—"and ideas your friends might talk about."

"Yeah, Mom. I think I understand what Dad's been talking about. While I have a few friends crazy about fashion, there's nobody seriously dieting or anything. I mean, just because someone prefers to drink Diet Coke doesn't mean they are on a diet, right?" Hannah teased, knowing that Diet Coke was Jennifer's favorite beverage of choice.

Jennifer chuckled at her daughter's gentle jab. "Right, Hannah. I've learned so much about this studying from the Bible with your dad. God's wisdom about food choices is quite different from what we hear from the world. Every diet plan I've ever heard restricts the choices of food you should eat. My friend from college would do a crash diet sometimes when she would only eat grapefruit and beets, with a few other tasty treats, for ten days." Hannah grimaced at the thought of grapefruit and beets. Her mother continued, "While she might have lost ten pounds for the moment, they sure didn't stay off, and the experience didn't change her eating habits that kept extra pounds on her frame the rest of the time."

"It seems like diets tell you, 'No, you can't have that.' After a while, I would get tired of that," Hannah said.

"The interesting thing is that the Bible never tells us that we may not eat any good thing that God created for our food, but God does want us to say 'No' to ourselves."

"What do you mean?" Hannah asked her mom.

"God made food for us to enjoy and for our nourishment. The flavors and variety should lead us to thank Him and praise Him for His goodness, His power, His creativity and His generosity. But God tells Christians that self-control is a good thing, that we should be busy serving and pleasing Him and other people, not indulging our every desire."

"So saying 'No' to yourself can be a good thing," Hannah concluded.

"Yes. I'll tell you, I've tried saying 'No' to myself a few times recently while making food choices. I never realized how self-indulgent I can be throughout the day. It's been a challenge, Hannah, to examine myself and see some sinful habits in areas that I have never considered before," Jennifer confessed.

"But Mom, you're not fat!" Hannah protested.

"Oh, but Hannah, that's not the point, is it?" Jennifer waited to let Hannah try to figure this out.

"So maybe I can't see the results of your bad eating habits in terms of your size," said Hannah thoughtfully, "but you still have a problem with gluttony?"

"Yes, Hannah, I do make sinful choices about eating food. I generally eat too much. I eat for my mouth and not for my stomach. Sometimes I eat trying to comfort my soul when food can't and won't make me happy."

"What do you mean, Mom, that you eat for your mouth?"

"Remember when we went to the mall yesterday afternoon? It was only an hour or two after lunch, and we really weren't hungry. But when we walked by the cinnamon rolls that smelled so warm and sweet, our mouths began to water, and we thought about getting one for a treat. Well, our stomach didn't signal us that we needed food for energy, did it?" Hannah shook her head. "It was our mouths signaling that our senses, our taste buds, wanted to be "tickled." That was a good opportunity for us to practice self-control. We said 'No' to our selfish desires."

"But that doesn't mean we should never eat cinnamon rolls, does it?" Hannah asked, a little confused.

"Certainly not!" Jennifer replied adamantly. "God is a good God, and He created yeast and sugar and cinnamon to be eaten and enjoyed, but at the right time, for the right reason, and for His glory, not to satisfy our hearts. You know that Bible verse, *'Whether then you eat or drink or whatever you do, do all to the glory of God.'* 1 Corinthians 10:31?"

"Yep. I even know a song for that verse," Hannah laughed, "but I think I'm starting to understand and appreciate it a little better."

"I'm so glad. I'm sure there will be other things to think about as our church works on this issue. Please come talk to me if you have any questions, OK, Hannah?" her Mom asked.

"Yes, Mom."

"And Hannah, will you help me? Will you keep me accountable in this area, especially when I'm tempted to eat for my mouth and not my stomach? It might be hard for me to hear, and I might not always respond in the right way, but God gave you to me as a blessing, and I think you're old enough to help your mom on this."

"Sure, Mom. I'll do my best to help you," Hannah agreed to this important assignment.

Eric took another approach to his Bible study this week. One of the first Bible passages about food Eric found was Genesis 2:15-16: *"Then the Lord God took the man and put him into the garden of Eden to cultivate it and keep it. The Lord God commanded the man, saying, "From any tree of the garden you may eat freely."*

Did this mean that God intended people to be vegetarian? Eric thought about some of his favorite foods, like last week's barbecued ribs with its finger-licking sauce. There was nothing better on a cold morning than to smell crispy bacon frying for breakfast. Thinking about the steam in his face as he carried the platter to the table, Eric remembered the Thanksgiving turkey that was savory and delicious, not just for that one meal, but for all the leftovers.

Before Eric left this passage to look for more in God's Word about eating meat, he considered a few other implications. First, Eric noted that God put man in the garden to cultivate it and keep it. Work. That was certainly the best way to build an appetite. Work also meant physical labor to burn up calories. Eric made note of the balance between working and eating.

Something else Eric noticed. God gave people freedom to eat from any tree of the garden, everything except for God's command in the next verse not to eat from the tree of the knowledge of good and evil. God had created so many different plants with different colors and flavors. Eric had to admit that sometimes he grumbled about eating his vegetables. And sometimes, especially when they were out at a restaurant, he avoided vegetables altogether. But there were probably lots of vegetables he had never tried. And this verse certainly included fruits. Was a tomato a fruit or a vegetable? What about cucumbers? He would have to ask his wife about that. God created such a variety.

Carbs were plant-based, too. Eric's olfactory nerves were tingling when he imagined the usual odors that wafted around Beverly's kitchen. Muffins. Cookies. Bread. Eric remembered those delicious smells even from the days when he was first dating Jennifer. He didn't mind waiting for her to finish getting ready for a date since Beverly insisted he enjoy her latest creation. A few times he had spoiled his dinner snacking on Beverly's baked goods. Bread made from grains of the field were an important part of meals, but they could also be a problem area for many people.

Before he ended his Bible study time, he wanted to find what God had to say about eating meat. He found something later in Genesis, after the flood of Noah. God said to Noah, *"Every moving thing that is alive shall be food for you; I give all to you, as I gave the green plant. Only you shall not eat flesh with its life, that is, its blood"* (Genesis 9:3-4). More to the point was God's vision to Peter in Acts 10:13, "A voice came to him, *"Get up, Peter, kill and eat!"* Good. There were clear instructions in the Bible to eat meat! In between these two messages, the people of Israel had been given rules about their diet to live separate from the world as God's chosen people. God had removed those restrictions for Jewish and Gentile believers after Christ came to earth.

"I really appreciate you taking me around town today, Ashley," said Cindy as she smiled at her new friend from the passenger seat of Ashley's GMC Terrain.

"My pleasure, Cindy. I just hope I don't forget to stop and show you the sights. I've lived here all of my life. Everything is so familiar that I might not notice it. Let's grab some lunch first. Are there any places you need to find?" Ashley asked as she started driving to Chik-fil-A.

"Well, I don't need a laundromat since we have a stacked washer and dryer right in our apartment, thank goodness. That's one of the hard things about moving around, finding where you can take your dirty laundry!" Cindy laughed. "And with all the baby stuff coming in, I really don't want to be hauling it down the street.

"I've found the Publix grocery store that seems to stock the same stuff at the same prices as the commissary on the Marine base," Cindy continued. "But I wouldn't mind knowing about any local secrets for fresh produce or good buys."

"I like to eat a lot of produce, too," said Ashley. "There's a Mexican grocery store across town that's worth the occasional drive. If you're on the outskirts of town, pick up the fresh produce from the farm stands. Right now, there are slim pickings for winter vegetables, so I don't often drive out, but they will be loaded with good stuff in a couple of months."

"I've seen some stands on the way to the Marine base, so maybe I'll stop one of these days. I wish they had a drive-through so I wouldn't have to get out of the car," she joked as she patted her belly.

"Speaking of getting out, here we are for lunch." And with that, the two young women headed inside the restaurant to order a good meal and enjoy each other's company.

As Ashley picked at her Cobb salad, Cindy polished off her grilled chicken sandwich, waffle fries, and fruit cup. Unfortunately, the peach shakes were not in season, so they both settled for iced tea.

"I know I'm using this pregnancy to eat a lot, but I really am hungry. They say I'm eating for two, but one of us is only five pounds and about a foot long. Aren't you hungry, Ashley?" Cindy asked when she noticed her friend wasn't eating much.

"Yes, I'm just a slow eater," explained Ashley. "Even though I'm hungry and I like this food, sometimes it's just hard for me to eat."

"Do you have a toothache or a stomach ache?" Cindy probed with concern.

"With all this talk about food and gluttony around the church, it's kind of ironic to talk about my food problems," began Ashley. "When I was a kid, I participated in gymnastics. I was pretty good, and my folks worked it out that I kept at it into high school. But by then, the pressure started getting pretty intense. Besides working out all the time and being highly competitive, eating was..." Ashley paused, looking for an appropriate way to explain it, "eating was not encouraged. When I started throwing up after every meal, that's when my mom looked for some help. Besides seeing a medical doctor, Chris' mom Jennifer started counseling me. She really helped me out by giving me a bigger perspective. When she shared the gospel with me, I eagerly believed in Jesus as my Lord and Savior. Then I could trust Him to help me make some changes. I dropped gymnastics and learned how to eat again, although it's a daily battle sometimes," she said as she gestured towards her salad. "I had to deal with some pretty mad people, including my coaches and my parents who got divorced around this same time, so spending time with Jennifer was really great. After a while, Chris started hanging around the house more when I was there with his mom. By the time we got around to dating, we were already good friends."

"Wow. Thanks for sharing that with me, Ashley. It's been a long time since I've had a close girlfriend to talk about stuff with. I'm always here to listen and help whenever you want to talk. And if I can help you eat that salad, I will!" Cindy joked again, just trying to lighten the mood. It worked, and Ashley laughed.

"Nope. I'll eat it. Why don't you get another drink while I finish this?"

"Are you trying to torture me? I've already gone to the bathroom twice with this baby sitting on my bladder. But I guess I will have another refill. Can I get you one?"

"Sure," replied Ashley as she picked up her fork to eat in earnest.

After lunch, the two friends went to the mall, which had every kind of store that Cindy could possibly need. Plus, while they walked around the mall, there were a lot of fun shops to check out, too. A couple of hours later, they extracted themselves from the mall with a few small shopping bags to go to Cindy's appointment.

"Thanks for driving me to my checkup at the Marine Base. Now it's my turn to show you around a territory that I'm familiar with. Even though I've never lived on this base, they all have some similarities, which sure helps families to get adjusted quickly." Cindy continued. "Besides moving around with Wayne for the past six years, we moved around with my dad in the military, too."

They found parking near the hospital entrance, and Cindy guided them through the building to the obstetrics department. Ashley sat in the waiting room with some old magazines while Cindy had her checkup. Ashley watched other pregnant women come in for their appointments. Her heart longed to join the ranks of these blessed wives. She was still thinking about this when Cindy came out a few minutes later.

"That didn't take too long. I've been coming in once a month, but now I'll be coming in every week until the baby's born," Cindy explained.

"Let me know if you need a ride again," offered Ashley.

As they climbed back into Ashley's Terrain, Cindy asked, "What about you and Chris? Are you planning to have kids?"

"Oh yes, we want to," Ashley said eagerly, "but nothing has happened yet. There could be some complications with getting pregnant from my eating disorder. So, we're just going to trust the Lord for His timing. We're also open to adoption. I pray a lot for patience," Ashley admitted.

"OK, I'll pray for you, too. I'm thankful for God's timing. Even though we wanted kids earlier, getting pregnant never happened before Wayne got deployed. Now he's around to enjoy every moment. But just wait until the baby comes. Wayne sleeps like a rock, so we'll see if he enjoys the midnight feedings!" Turning to her friend one more time, Cindy said sheepishly, "How about a snack before we head for home? There's a great ice cream place on the base."

Chapter 15

Beverly met her accountability partner one afternoon at the nail salon for pedicures. Since Stephany worked at a school, she was available for a few hours in the afternoon while her children participated in after-school enrichment activities.

"Thank you," said Stephany as she sat in the lounge chair next to Beverly as the treatment began. "This is a real treat for me. In fact, I don't think I've ever had a professional pedicure. I hope I'm not too ticklish," she giggled.

"Oh, my, I agree it is a luxury, but something I love to do, getting pedicures. My husband encourages me to do it. He's always been romantic and likes to take me out on dates. Most of my evening shoes show my toes, and I want to be ready any time he wants to go out!" As Beverly explained her reasons, Stephany's face drooped as she considered her unromantic, broken marriage.

Beverly continued, "Getting pedicures has also been a good activity to share with my daughter Jennifer and my daughter-in-law when she's in town. The fun was extended when my granddaughter Hannah finally got old enough to enjoy the treat, and now I have a few sweet young ladies married to my grandsons who join me, too. But only one of them, Ashley, lives in town."

This all sounded like a fun family activity to Stephany. "I'll have to find a special activity like this to do with my daughters as they get older," said Stephany thoughtfully.

"Back in the early days, we just painted each other's toenails at home. But now it's a girls-day-out extravaganza!" exclaimed Beverly, which revealed how much she enjoyed the event.

"What color will you have today, Beverly?" the familiar attendant asked after she had finished the cleaning and massage.

"Something in the red-orange spectrum, please," she replied politely before turning back to Stephany. "I don't really care for orange, but my husband likes it. Between you and me, I'll admit that I can't really see my toes anyway." Had Beverly actually admitted that? Yes, she had revealed her secret: she was too plump to see her toes.

When she arrived home after her pedicure with Stephany, Beverly pulled out her notes from Eric's sermon as well as the worksheet that Bill Sanderson had created about mortifying sin. Could this list of questions really help her to understand her own sinful behavior so that she could stop and change it? Could this make a difference? Well, Beverly believed that God's Word was sufficient to address every aspect of life. She knew that she could not change her behavior by her own strength. She had proven that many times over the years. When she prayed this afternoon, she asked for God's wisdom and renewed strength to try again. She also remembered to pray for her accountability partner Stephany who had promised to look at the worksheet today, too.

Beverly chose to evaluate an eating binge she had a few weeks ago when she was home alone in the evening. She could barely think of everything she ate, but she remembered feeling stuffed and sick by the time she went to bed, her stomach bloated and ankles swollen, but that was after hours of putting food into her mouth. When Leonard had left the house that afternoon to help an old buddy work on his model train display for a few hours, she started snacking on the leftover baked goods she had made for his friends. She had been smelling their warm brown sugar fragrance all afternoon. How many had there been left over? Over a dozen. How many muffins had she eaten? All of them. She had planned to take them as a gift for a sick friend from church, but by the time she got through with her binge, there was nothing left to take.

When she had cooked dinner that night, she prepared a full, nutritious, well-balanced meal, enough for two people, as if Leonard would be joining her even though she knew he would be playing with the train set well into the night. Although she had served herself a regular portion on her plate to start with, she kept going back for more until she had eaten both portions. Then came dessert. She decided to treat herself to a few frozen cream puffs, but she couldn't seem to stop at just a few. She finished the whole family-sized box. That was a summary of what she had eaten in one night, but it looked more like a grocery list for a large party.

The second question on the evaluation worksheet for mortifying sin was to write down what she had been thinking during that eating binge. After spending most days with Leonard since his retirement, she thought she would feel relieved and free while he has gone that evening, but really she felt lonely. It reminded her how lonely she had been as a child. Back then, when she was poor, she had been left alone with no food in the house. She couldn't eat, but she remembered doing things she wasn't supposed to do, like watching inappropriate TV shows for hours.

Reviewing her eating binge, she remembered thinking that her actions would not be seen by anyone else, so it seemed like her overindulging was her little secret, like watching those shows she wasn't allowed to as a child. She thought that it didn't hurt anyone else, did it? She had told herself at the time that the baked goods would be comforting while she was alone, but instead, they made her uncomfortable physically. Worse yet, it dulled her heart towards loving others. Not only did she have nothing to give away, she felt too sick and lazy to go out and visit her friend. At dinner, she kept going back for more helpings because, well, because she could. There was no one to stop her, not even herself. Dessert was supposed to be a "pat on the back," her reward for all her hard work that day. But had she done anything to deserve a whole box of cream puffs? She answered that question out loud: "No."

Purposefully evaluating the incident now, Beverly recognized that on that evening, she had not engaged her mind or will at all. She had been making choices based on her emotions and feelings, not on reason or wisdom. So now, after just two questions on the evaluation form, Beverly could truthfully conclude that her actions were, in fact, rooted in the sin of gluttony, indulging in too much food for the wrong reasons. Gluttony was surrounded by the sins of selfishness, laziness, pride, fear, and greed. Tears streamed down her face, and she bowed her head in shame. She was as alone right now as she had been the night of the food binge. Yet she knew that during both nights, God had always been present. God had seen it all. God knew it would happen because He knew she was a sinner at heart. So God had sent His Son Jesus to save sinners like her. God inspired the writers of Scripture to explain how He could not only forgive sin but empower believers to stop sinning! Even though she had started this study time in prayer, she interrupted her project to pray again, confessing and repenting, asking again for His wisdom and His comfort.

There was more work for her to do. She looked back on her journaling, shocked at what she had written, yet knowing that it was accurate. She could see some sinful thoughts and behavior but needed help identifying them with accurate Bible words for the sin. The second week of the accountability plan was to study God's Word. That's exactly what she was going to do to fill her mind with God's truth to continue to mortify the sin of gluttony.

Chapter 16

Pastor Eric hosted an informal meeting with a few members of his congregation who were participating in the accountability program. They discussed some of the activities they had enjoyed so far including purposefully praying, not just for their accountability partners but for others in the church. A group of young ladies asked for prayer for their friend Giselle who, although she refused to participate in the program, was watching the people involved with interest. Karen gave her testimony of salvation, how her friend Elizabeth had presented the gospel after Pastor Eric's sermon about gluttony, and so Giselle's friends were encouraged to pray all the more. Many members were enthusiastic about the fitness class that Wayne Long was teaching on Saturdays. Eric revealed some of the activities to come, seeking their input, before returning to the topic of studying God's Word for wisdom and understanding.

"It's exciting for me to hear how people are studying the Bible on their own and with their accountability partners. That was the idea for the second week of the accountability program, and I am rejoicing to see how God is working in our congregation. Keep it up. In week seven I hope you all return to your Bibles with renewed enthusiasm. I've seen some of you sharing notes about what you've learned from God's Word, not just about gluttony, but also after Sunday sermons and from your personal studies about your daily walk with the Lord. Let me share with you a couple of verses of encouragement and challenge that I recently read from Romans 12. Verses 10-13 reads, '*Be devoted to one another in brotherly love; give preference to one another in honor; not lagging behind in diligence, fervent in spirit, serving the Lord; rejoicing in hope, persevering in tribulation, devoted to prayer, contributing to the needs of the saints, practicing hospitality.*'

"We are in a spiritual battle, and God has not put us there alone. We are part of His church, the body of Christ. While we are individually struggling, failing and winning, we are in the midst of other people in the same battle as well. So be sure to look around for other people to help. Love them, like that verse says. Honor and prefer others. Pray for them. Practice hospitality by inviting someone over for a meal to show them what you've been working on regarding portion size or nutrition." Some laughed at this idea even while they considered how to do it.

"Let's also keep 1 Thessalonians 5:14 in mind," said Eric in conclusion. "I think I did a pretty thorough job of admonishing the unruly, so let's work together to encourage the fainthearted, help the weak, and be patient with everyone. Thanks, everyone. Have a great week!"

Karen and Elizabeth had planned to go out to dinner after the meeting with Pastor Eric. As two young working women, eating out was a regular part of their routines and a good opportunity to socialize. When they got out to their car, they started to talk about places to go, but then another topic arose.

"Karen, Pastor Eric mentioned in the meeting portion sizes. I know that gluttony includes eating too much at meals. But to be honest, I don't really know what the right portion sizes look like," Elizabeth admitted.

"I know what you mean," Karen agreed. "I think the amounts of food that we get served at many restaurants are way too big, but I've always tried to clean my plate."

"Yes, restaurants do pile on the food and charge a big price to match. And sometimes I think the plate size and shape can be deceiving, too," said Elizabeth.

"Well, we'll probably have to do some practical research at home in our kitchens, but I still want to go out tonight. What shall we do?" asked Karen, and she started her car.

"Let's split!" suggested Elizabeth.

"Yes, we'll go, but where?" asked Karen.

"No, what I mean is let's split a meal when we get to the restaurant. We both know that the portion is probably too big for one person. So, let's eat half. That means we can also split the bill," suggested Elizabeth.

"I like that idea. I wonder how much money we'll save?" pondered Karen. "And let's figure out which older woman from church we can talk to about proper portion sizes."

The next time Beverly met with Stephany was not in the glamorous beauty parlor but in Stephany's own living room. There were no bright lights, no noisy hum of chit-chat, no pungent odor of nail polish. Stephany's home was a second-floor apartment furnished with well-used but comfortable pieces that, while they were not color- and pattern-coordinated, fit nicely into the space without being crowded or cluttered. The place was tidy with toys discreetly gathered in baskets and bins around the room and peeking out from under the sofa. The room was a little dim, but it was warm and quiet. The children would be coming home from after-school activities in two hours, so Beverly had agreed to meet Stephany for Bible study and prayer at her convenience.

After they reviewed and updated their prayer requests from the last time they met, they spent a few minutes in prayer together. Beverly praised the Lord for who He was and what He had done for them this week and for His generous gift of salvation. Then she confessed her sin generally, not getting into too much detail, but admitting in prayer to God of eating too much for the wrong reasons this week, and admitting to some of the sinful reasons behind her eating, such as pride, selfishness, and greed. Thanking God for his forgiveness of these sins, she asked for His help to put on righteousness instead. Beverly also asked for wisdom and strength for Stephany as she raised her children, maintained a peaceful relationship with her ex-husband, worked hard and made personal eating choices to glorify God.

When Beverly finished her powerful and extensive prayer, Stephany could barely speak to ask God to care for and bless Beverly. After the amen, Stephany looked up into Beverly's eyes.

"You sound like an expert in prayer," Stephany commented.

"Well, honey, I've been praying to God for many, many years. There are two things I have learned to help me when I pray to God. The first thing that helps me pray is my Bible. It's full of the right words when I don't know what to say. The second help is an old acronym, ACTS. That stands for Adoration, Confession, Thanksgiving, and Supplication. That helps me to keep my prayer focused on God, not me and my needs," explained Beverly.

"How does the Bible help you? I didn't hear you reading a passage or even quoting a Bible verse when you prayed," asked Stephany.

"Sometimes I do that, read and pray through a passage or quote a verse word for word. But the Bible informs my prayer. I think that's the idea Pastor Eric wants to encourage this week as we study the Bible in our accountability groups. Rather than Eric just telling us what the Bible says about food and eating and sin, he wants us to discover it, pray about it, and apply it to ourselves. Do you want to get started?" prompted Beverly.

"Yes, but before you leave, I want to hear more about the ACTS prayer acronym," said Stephany.

Beverly and Stephany pulled out their Bibles, notebooks, and the worksheet about mortifying sin. Beverly decided to share with Stephany the results of her efforts to examine herself. While Stephany was surprised by Beverly's transparency, she was also surprised to recognize some of the same problems she had faced on many late nights when she was alone and sad.

"So I'm now ready to work on steps three and four to find Bible words that identify my sin and the things that I should put off. Will you help me with this?" asked Beverly with humility.

Reading through Beverly's account of the situation, the ladies agreed that while Beverly had a good plan to take the leftover muffins to a sick friend, she selfishly chose to eat them all. Her good plan was overruled by selfish action. Being alone at the time, Beverly had had no accountability or encouragement to move into action with her good idea. Perhaps there was some laziness in her desire not to go through the trouble of packaging the gift, calling and driving over to visit her friend.

Regarding her feeling of loneliness, Stephany could certainly relate. The divorce had led to many lonely hours not just with the absence of her spouse, but also the days when the children spent time with their father. Both women acknowledged that they tried to comfort themselves with food during these times of loneliness.

"But food's not going to help us stop feeling lonely, is it?" observed Stephany.

"No. It never has and it never will. So, we'd better stop trying to do that," resolved Beverly.

When it came to her dinner experience, Beverly had had a good idea to serve herself one portion, but then what happened to thwart that good intention? First, more food was readily available. Why had she cooked so much food? Did she already intend to eat too much? That was being selfish and greedy. Next time she cooked like that, she could immediately wrap it up and store it in the refrigerator or freezer.

"And the award for the greatest person of the day goes to Beverly. Here is your trophy full of cream puffs!" Although she said it jokingly, they instantly recognized how foolish it sounded that Beverly rewarded herself with cream puffs. Beverly and Stephany laughed, both shaking their heads.

"That's pride, right?" Stephany attempted to identify the sinful action with a Bible word.

"That's pride all right," Beverly agreed. "Who do I think I am? Even if I had done a few good things that day, I didn't deserve a reward for doing anything special. Being kind to others is only doing what I ought to do as a Christian. And remember, I had just eaten my good idea of delivering a gift to a sick friend. I didn't deserve a pat on the back; I deserved a swat on the... well, maybe a slap on the hand!"

"So we've figured out a lot of Bible words for what we should put off," Stephany summarized, "but what should we put on?"

"OK. I know you're a list-maker just like me, so let's make a two-column list. One side will be the sins we've identified. The other list will be things we find from Scripture that we should put on instead," instructed Beverly. Stephany liked that idea and pulled out two Steno notebooks that already had a line down the middle of each page.

Next to "selfish," they wrote "selfless" and "serve others." Beverly started talking about all the people she knew who needed help and encouragement. Starting small, Stephany recognized that she could serve her children and ex-husband better. She would start looking for more people at work or in her extended family who could use help and encouragement.

Next to "lazy," they wrote "work heartily as unto the Lord" and "get moving." Both ladies recognized that in the dark evenings, they were tempted to sit down after a long day. They came up with a list of quiet activities they could work on, such as crafts or writing notes or making calls. They challenged each other to do one more activity after dinner before settling down, such as putting on a load of laundry, cleaning something, or packing lunches for the next day.

Next to "seek comfort in food," they wrote, "seek comfort from God and people." Looking around her living room, Stephany decided to clear off the table next to her rocking chair in order to set her Bible there for easy access. Remembering how much she loved to sing, she checked her stereo and loaded a set of praise and worship CDs. The ladies promised to call each other on lonely evenings now that they were friends.

Next to "reward self," they wrote, "give glory to whom glory is due." Beverly quickly sketched something on a fresh piece of paper in her notebook. "The next time I'm tempted to reward myself for doing good, I'm going to take a look at this." Beverly turned her notebook so that Stephany could see her sketch of Jesus' cross.

More Bible study would be necessary to gather verses to help them put off wrong thoughts and feelings and put on truth and encouragement. They agreed to share what they discovered over the next few weeks. After this intense spiritual discussion, Stephany changed the subject to a practical application. "Pastor Eric challenged us to eat less and exercise more. I'm learning a lot about exercise on Saturday mornings with Wayne's extreme Marine fitness program," said Stephany. "But how do I know how much or little to eat? I don't think my stomach can tell me when to stop anymore."

"Unfortunately, Stephany, we have overridden our stomach's signal to stop for so long that we are dull to it. It's like our conscience. God created us in His image to know right and wrong, but when we keep sinning and telling ourselves we're still OK, we lose that guilty conscience that God gave us for our benefit."

"Wow. I never thought about it that way," replied Stephany.

"Maybe we should try to find and listen to our full signal again," suggested Beverly thoughtfully.

"How do we do that?" asked Stephany.

"We live in a country with such a bounty of food available, I doubt if we've truly felt hungry in years. In the Bible, we read about people fasting and praying. Now there's a right way and a wrong way to fast according to the Bible. It has to do with our attitude and motivation, a desire to set ourselves apart for worship. In contrast, the Pharisees hypocritically paraded themselves when they fasted to bring attention to themselves.

"We could try skipping a meal and spending that time in Bible study. Then we could listen for our tummies to grumble!" said Beverly with a laugh.

"Let's do it together when we meet next week at lunch time," suggested Stephany, and they set a date to fast.

Chapter 17

Pastor Eric continued to dedicate himself and his congregation to the Lord in prayer and turn to His Word for wisdom. He was confident that Scripture had direction and answers for him as he led his congregation, remembering 1 Corinthians 10:13: *"No temptation has overtaken you but such as is common to man; and God is faithful, who will not allow you to be tempted beyond what you are able, but with the temptation will provide the way of escape also, that you will be able to endure it."* Today, Eric wanted to learn more about his role in ministering to people struggling with the sin of gluttony. Was it his place as a pastor, as a friend, and as a family member to encourage other people to eat less food? What was the best way to talk about this subject? The Bible could answer these questions.

Today, Eric was studying Galatians 5. The apostle Paul was pastoring the church in Galatia, giving them encouragement and instructions on living the godly life, with plenty of exhortation and warnings mixed in. Starting in verse sixteen, Paul was exhorting his congregation to strive against sin, contrasting walking in the Spirit with a list of deeds of the flesh. Eric noted that Paul explained that everyone struggles with sin, but that it is a believer's duty to strive against sin and to develop the fruit of righteousness. Eric had certainly been talking to the accountability groups about striving against sin. From Paul's list of fruit, Eric wanted to study more about developing self-control since it seemed to directly relate to the issues the members were facing.

The Greek root of this word, translated self-control or temperance in older translations, was a noun which meant the virtue of one who masters his desires and passions, especially the sensual appetite, which would include food and drink. An older dictionary defined temperance as restraint in food and drink so as not to be excessive or immoderate. This word seemed to describe the attitude and actions his congregation was striving for. So how could someone develop and practice self-control? While he could teach them these truths from Scripture, Pastor Eric recognized that individuals would have to act to control themselves. His accountability program, or any other program, no matter how structured or entertaining they were, would always fail if a person would not control themselves.

So, Eric decided he would present this information to the accountability groups and then brainstorm lots of actions that they could take to practice self-control. These ideas could be as simple as using a smaller plate at each meal or writing out the portion sizes they would allow themselves before they ate. Or they could be more drastic, such as talking to themselves out loud when tempted to eat for the wrong reasons, telling themselves to go read the Bible for comfort instead of food and reciting a Bible verse of truth to calm them during a stressful time. After all, in verse 24 of Galatians 5, Paul wrote that Christians took drastic measures to deal with their sin, using the imagery of crucifying the fleshly passions and desires.

In conclusion, Eric determined that it was OK for him as their loving pastor to talk to them about eating less, but it was important that they took responsibility to learn and exercise self-control over their eating choices.

"Hi, Honey! Welcome home," Jennifer greeted Eric cheerfully as she wiped her hands on the kitchen towel and walked around the kitchen island where she had been fixing dinner. She barely got her arms around him for a hug before more arms were entangled around their waists.

"Hey, Dad. I'm glad you're home!" interrupted Samuel. "I've been working on my safari report from school. You should see what I've learned about African animals."

"I have a feeling you are going to update me on all your research, son," Eric gently laughed at his son's enthusiasm. "But let me give my wife a kiss and wash my hands before dinner. Will you please help your mom set the table? Then we can talk about your wild animals at dinner."

Samuel was not deterred from his enthusiasm to update his Dad about his report. He quietly set the table and filled each glass with everyone's favorite beverage. He surveyed the dinner options as he helped his mom put several hot and cold dishes in the center of the table. One juicy steak was cut into strips; Samuel knew he could eat two strips himself. The mashed potatoes looked lumpy but colorful as if confetti had been sprinkled in. His mom liked to add other vegetables into the mix like carrots and peas or spinach, but Samuel didn't mind as long as there was plenty of butter. His mom carefully poured some vinaigrette dressing on the salad, so Samuel gave it a toss with the wooden spoons before carrying it over to the table. At his mom's instruction, Samuel raided the refrigerator for a bowl of sliced, tart Granny Smith apples.

"How come these apples are still white on the insides?" Samuel asked when he extracted himself and the bowl from the cold refrigerator.

"I pour a little orange juice on them right after I cut them. Oranges have citric acid which keeps the fruit looking good, at least for a few minutes until you eat them all!" Jennifer teased her son. "I want to serve them with these cheddar cheese cubes and walnuts."

When Eric returned to the kitchen area from washing his hands, Hannah followed in tow. The family sat down around the dinner table and bowed their heads while Eric offered a prayer of thanksgiving to the Lord.

"OK, Samuel, astonish me with some animal facts, buddy!" said Eric after the food had been passed around.

"Well, Dad, the first thing I learned for my report on African animals is that there are no tigers in Africa!" Samuel waited for everyone's jaw to drop. When he saw that no one was too shocked to eat, he continued. "Tigers are only in Asia, mostly in Siberia and India, although there aren't many left in the wild anymore. So, I'm not going to research tigers anymore. I'll work on some different animals tomorrow, but the first thing I'm going to do before getting excited about an animal is to check to see if it even lives in Africa!" Everyone chuckled at Samuel's good idea for his continued research.

"I have an interesting question based on my research about food," announced Eric. His family braced themselves as they anticipated a deeply spiritual discussion ahead. "What's the difference between a fruit and a vegetable?"

"Is this a joke, Dad?" asked Hannah warily.

"No, no. I've been thinking about food portions and nutrition, considering some Bible verses, and for my own mind's clarity, who can tell me the difference?"

"Fruits are sweet and delicious, and vegetables are anything your mom forces you to eat because she says it's healthy for you," suggested Samuel with a sly grin at his mother. She smiled back, knowing that she had very little confrontations at the table with her children about eating vegetables. But then again she tended to serve vegetables that she liked to eat: spinach salad, broccoli, artichokes, peas and corn, and carrots and cucumber with ranch dip.

"We studied this in health class last year. Fruits are the part of the plant that protects the seed, and vegetables are any other parts of the plant that we eat," explained Hannah succinctly.

"Huh," Eric interjected. "That's a simple definition, but it makes a lot of sense. Obviously, apples are fruits that surround the core full of seeds," he said as he looked at the apple slice he held between his fingers before taking a bite. "But carrots are the underground roots of that plant, so carrots are vegetables."

"So that definition is clear enough to end the age-old dispute whether a tomato is a fruit or a vegetable," chimed in Jennifer. "Tomatoes have seeds inside, so it is a fruit."

"What about pumpkin?" asked Samuel with a bit of concern. "Are you telling me that pumpkin is a fruit? I thought that was the best vegetable at Thanksgiving."

"By my definition, it's a fruit, Samuel," explained Hannah to her disappointed brother.

"What's broccoli?" asked Samuel trying to sort out whether he should continue making such an effort to eat broccoli or not.

"It's a good green vegetable, Samuel," said his mom. "We eat the flower of the broccoli plant. And some people eat more of the plant, the leaves, as broccoli greens. My favorite vegetables, artichokes, are the flowers of that plant. If you don't pick them in time, they burst open with bright purple fuzz in the center of them."

With a twinkling grin at her family, the teenager Hannah protested, "Please don't ever send me a floral bouquet of broccoli and artichoke florets!"

Later that evening, Jennifer joined Eric on the sofa. She sat close enough for him to wrap his arm around her, but in a good position to see his face while they talked. She asked him about his other research about food.

"I've been working on a plan for the fifth-week activity which is supposed to feature fruit. The passage in Colossians refers to a believer bearing fruit. It is parallel to the two phrases that come before it where it says to walk worthy and please God. When I think about fruit in the Bible, I often think of the verses about the fruit of the Spirit. Let's look it up so we can get it right." When he paused, Jennifer stood up to grab the closest Bible.

She looked up Galatians 5:22-23 and began to read. *"But the fruit of the Spirit is love, joy, peace, patience, kindness, goodness, faithfulness, gentleness, self-control; against such things there is no law."*

Eric began to explain that these verses directly followed a passage about putting off sin. He also pointed out that there was only a single piece of fruit in the verse. "That means that the list that follows contains a variety of characteristics of one thing. When the Holy Spirit is active in a believer's life, they will be characterized by love, and joy, and peace, and patience, and all the others. Now as sinners, we're not going to have any of these perfected, but I think that sometimes we stick to the areas that we're good at. This is a good reminder that God wants to round us out in all of these areas. I know that our studies recently have challenged most of us in the area of self-control.

"I think this will be a great passage to discuss and memorize with the accountability groups. But I think this might be a good opportunity to lighten things up a bit and have some fun," said Eric.

"What did you have in mind?" Jennifer asked a little warily.

"How about a creative contest to design one piece of fruit to represent all of the characteristics? You know, don't just paint a round orange, but make a new piece of fruit in a new shape, with an unusual color on a never-seen-before style of tree." As Eric explained his first idea, Jennifer came up with a few of her own.

"What about fruit juggling? It's a good eye-hand coordination challenge, and I heard Wayne say that he's tried it in his after-school fitness classes for an indoor activity. Kids get pretty worked up about it." They laughed at the thought of their congregation juggling fruit around the church. "To avoid the mess, we'd better start with handkerchiefs or beanbags."

"I was looking around about fruit harvesting in our area," Eric continued. "Strawberries will be available for picking starting near the end of March. We'll have to wait for summertime before the peaches are ready."

Jennifer added more to his idea. "Maybe this could be a church-wide event, a spring picnic to include other friends and family members who aren't doing the accountability project. It would be an opportunity to show some of the skeptics that we still appreciate God's wonderful variety of food that He created. Now that some of the accountability partners have really teamed up they might like to coordinate this event as a service project."

"Do you have someone in mind who might be able to coordinate the spring picnic?" Eric asked, knowing full well that neither of them could take it on right now.

"Betsy Merriwether is always a great organizer, and I know she feels out of the loop since her husband Stan is really antagonistic about the gluttony project. The picnic might be just the thing for Betsy to serve the church, along with Nadia Saint and their women's ministry friends. I think my mom and her partner Stephany might enjoy the project since they've become quite a team. Let's see...there is also that enthusiastic pair, Karen and Elizabeth, and this picnic project might be something Sarah can invite her friend Giselle to help with, since she's been avoiding the other activities. Even though Ashley and Wayne's wife Cindy aren't doing the accountability project either, they might like to help out, at least before Cindy has the baby. It might be fun for Ashley to get involved in something while Cindy's busy with the baby and her family for a while." Eric liked all of Jennifer's suggestions, so he asked her to call them to set up a planning meeting soon.

Chapter 18

Stephany called Beverly, not in crisis but in triumph. "I had a good day today, Beverly. I sat down in my chair several times today and read those Bible verses we've been talking about instead of seeking comfort in food. God gave me a special opportunity today because of it."

"What happened?" Beverly asked curiously.

"I was sitting there when my daughter Carmen ran to me in tears because of something her sister did to provoke her. Because I was full up with Scripture, I had words of wisdom to offer her for comfort," she explained, "and for correction. She returned to play with her sister with a much better attitude, and we enjoyed a peaceful evening together. I thought of this Bible verse, 2 Corinthians 1:3-4: *'Blessed be the God and Father of our Lord Jesus Christ, the Father of mercies and God of all comfort, who comforts us in all our affliction so that we will be able to comfort those who are in any affliction with the comfort with which we ourselves are comforted by God.'"*

"That is a comforting passage, for sure. How many times did you read the word *comfort?"* Beverly asked.

"Five times I read the word *comfort*. This passage is full of God's blessing and mercy," explained Stephany as she looked through the verses again.

"Thanks for sharing this with me today, Stephany. I have been comforted by this Scripture today, too," Beverly said as she closed their telephone conversation.

Wayne did not miss one exercise class. On one Saturday in March, he was an enthusiastic teacher and husband. On the next Saturday, he was a sleep-deprived, slightly confused daddy. Between those dates, his wife Cindy had given birth to a bouncing baby boy. She was home and doing well. After a few days at home together, Cindy had encouraged Wayne to keep his commitment to the exercise class. She thought it would do him good to burn off some energy after the initial confusion most first-time parents face.

Although a little groggy, Wayne had a smile on his face and lots of enthusiasm to encourage the members of his class. After they enjoyed the exercises he had planned for the morning, they gathered around Wayne with some fitness-related questions.

"Wayne, I have really enjoyed getting outside and walking. But you know that we've been getting a lot of rain, and sometimes I get busy during the day and don't think about exercising until the evening when it's too dark to walk outside. Do you think I should invest in a treadmill? Or do you have any other suggestions?" asked one of the faithful walkers from his class.

"That's a good question. I never recommend buying an expensive piece of equipment until you've done a lot of research and have proven to yourself that you will use it. That's why there are so many good deals at yard sales on used exercise equipment; they haven't been used!" Everyone joined Wayne in a little laugh about this fitness and financial truism. "I've tried to show you a variety of exercises that you can do in your own home without fancy equipment. But sometimes we need some other motivation when we are in comfortable, familiar surroundings with the comfy sofa behind you and the kitchen right around the corner. One great way to get motivated is to make plans to exercise with someone else. Work out with your spouse or your kids. Or invite your accountability partner over. Or if you know someone who lives near you or moves at the same pace as you in class, call them up to exercise before sharing a meal in fellowship.

"If you want to invest a little bit of money, I recommend starting with small items like light weights or resistance bands, or fun fitness DVDs like Leslie Sansone's walking exercise program for beginners. Leslie's aerobic routines are based on walking in place, or marching if you men want to call it that, and utilize some basic moves, not dance steps, to get people moving. One feature is that she divides each DVD into miles or minutes, so with only one DVD, you can decide how long you want to exercise, then change it up easily for variety if you're stuck inside for several days. My wife Cindy likes these routines and can do a pretty good imitation of Leslie Sansone. I'll bring one next week to class, and we'll do a routine," offered Wayne, and his class seemed happy to take him up on the offer.

"How long should I be exercising? And how many days a week do I have to exercise?" came another question from a class member.

"It is most productive if you can exercise for at least thirty minutes with your heart rate elevated. Real and effective cardiovascular aerobic exercise should cause you to breathe more and maybe even sweat. Remember to start with a warm-up before challenging your heart at a high rate, then return to normal breathing as you cool down and stretch. Since many people no longer get this quality and quantity of exercise in their normal work day, we should purposefully exercise at least three times a week for general good health. Since many in our group are trying to lose weight, then you should strive to be exercising at least five times per week."

"I thought it was unsafe to exercise every day," someone commented.

"What you're probably thinking of is muscle strain from strength training. It is recommended that you do strength training every other day to give your body time to rebuild the muscle fibers. But your heart wants to be challenged every day. Some of you have started with fifteen minutes at a time, and that's a great place to start. Let's start pushing it, either increasing the time or doing two workouts a day until you can go thirty minutes in one session. You are all able to do that much and more with me on Saturdays, you know," Wayne chided them gently.

"We'll be learning about strength training in a few weeks," Wayne continued. "Remember to bring canned food to donate to Harvest Hope on that day. Next week, Pastor Eric wants me to teach you juggling!" Everyone laughed at the idea but murmured to each other that they would give it a try. In closing, Wayne said, "Our class is over for the morning, but it's a beautiful day outside. Anyone want to exercise longer and go for a walk?" Many people walked out of the class, out to enjoy a walk with friends on a beautiful day.

Chapter 19

Eric Harvey and Nick Saint had met several times over the past few weeks ever since they had become accountability partners. Once Nick got over the silly idea that he could not be friends with his pastor, they had productive meetings to get to know each other and to address the issue at hand, gluttony. Eric's family was delighted when they heard that Nick and his wife Nadia would be coming over for dinner. Who wouldn't get excited about showing hospitality to Santa?

After dinner, Samuel timidly approached Nick Saint, which was an unusual posture for Samuel to take since he had known Nick all his life from church. While it was not a surprise to see a man who looked like Santa Claus sitting in the congregation, its novelty had still not worn off for Samuel. Especially now since he had a few burning questions for Nick.

"Mr. Saint, I have a proposition for you," Samuel finally said.

"What's the deal, Samuel?" Nick responded curiously.

"I will let you pull my hair if you will let me tug on your beard. Not too hard, though. I promise."

Nick was surprised by the request but thought it was reasonable, so he settled himself in one of the comfortable recliners in the Harveys' den and prepared himself. Samuel grabbed a small fistful of Nick's beard and gave it a gentle tug. He was surprised to feel how thick it was, as well as how soft. And of course, it was firmly attached to Nick's chin.

"I thought it would feel more wiry," Samuel observed.

"I try to keep it conditioned. That way my face doesn't feel itchy all the time to me, and my wife will still kiss me!" Nick joked. Rather than pulling Samuel's hair pursuant to the deal, Nick playfully ruffled Samuel's head to mess up his hair instead. "So why did you want to pull my beard, Samuel?" Nick noticed that Hannah had been observing the proceedings from the doorway.

"I didn't hurt you, did I? Good. I didn't do it to cause you pain. I'm sure you get kids sitting on your lap pulling your beard just to be mean." Nick chuckled at this true statement. Samuel continued, "I wanted to pull your beard because I was curious. You are a real man, and I see you at church worshipping God like a real Christian, but you look like this make-believe character from the world."

"That's a great observation, Samuel. And that's something I have thought about ever since I became a Christian. I believe that the heart of Christmas is the opportunity to proclaim the birth of Jesus Christ, the Son of God who became a man so that He could save His people from their sin. So, you are probably wondering how I can participate in the world's presentation of the character of Santa Claus which often distracts from the true focus of Christmas, right?" Samuel nodded, and Hannah came over to listen closely to the response.

"First, I strongly believe that it is wrong for parents to lie to their children about who Santa Claus is. The ninth commandment tells us that lying is a sin. I know from raising our children that, at a very young age, they could tell the difference between real and make-believe. We wanted to always tell our daughters the truth about everything so that they would trust us as honest, wise counsel throughout their lives. And that trust had to start at a very young age. The biggest issue of all was to be clear to always present Jesus Christ as a real person in history and eternity, with all His teaching, miracles, and powers, as well as the special details of His birth, His death, and His resurrection.

"We also told our children the truth about Santa Claus, that Santa is a make-believe character from a fictional story. That's really not too hard for any child to understand. It was probably easier for them to understand since it was their regular ol' dad who lived with them every day but only dressed up as Santa in December. Knowing that Santa is make-believe does not take the fun out of dressing up and giving presents and talking about Santa. My girls have dressed up and enjoyed some of the opportunities that I have had to show love and kindness to a variety of people in a variety of circumstances. Besides the personal appearances I make for money, I voluntarily take toys to orphans. I also visit widows and other elderly people who don't get many visits in their retirement home. At any age, people's faces light up to see Santa, even though they all know perfectly well that I'm a regular guy dressed up like a make-believe character. And I have had many opportunities to present the gospel of Jesus Christ while wearing my Santa costume!"

This was quite a new perspective for Samuel and Hannah to consider. They sat there in wonder at Nick because of his testimony of the Lord Jesus Christ, not because of the frivolous character he portrayed.

"Please don't get him started on the legends surrounding the historical figure of Nicholas, a bishop in the Christian church back in 400 A.D.," teased Mrs. Saint as she walked into the den after helping Jennifer tidy up the kitchen after dinner.

Samuel and Hannah looked at Nick expectantly, but he stood up, ready to go. "Another story for another time, Samuel and Hannah. Or better yet, do some of your own research."

When Nick met with Pastor Eric a few days later for coffee, he told Eric about the conversation with his children.

"Samuel actually pulled your beard?" Eric asked incredulously.

"Yes, but not too hard," assured Nick.

"I'm kind of jealous...but I won't even try to do it," said Eric. "I'll just ask you this: how is your Bible study going?"

"This has been a great assignment, Pastor Eric, to evaluate our sin issues, looking for what to put off and finding something in Scripture that we should put on. Once I finish these notes, I'll be better prepared with the Word of God the next time I am challenged to eat in a self-glorifying way."

"That's a good perspective, Nick. So, what did you find out?"

Nick began to review his notes. When he and Eric had talked in the past, they agreed that they struggled in a few common areas: snacking for the wrong reasons and taking portions that were too big. Snacking was really an escape to the kitchen cupboard when they were worried about something. They often grabbed chips, cookies, or other conveniently packaged junk food, and mindlessly shoveled handfuls into their mouths, barely tasting the flavors, often while staring at something on television to forget about their worries for a while. Nick explained his habit of snacking at work when there were lulls in the action. Nick clearly consumed calories when he was bored at work, and Eric began to wonder if he had that habit as well, although he didn't take a lunch box full of snacks with him.

"So we definitely discovered that we snack for the wrong reasons. Those reasons include trying to comfort ourselves during times of worry and trying to entertain ourselves when we're bored," said Eric, and Nick nodded his head in agreement. "So what remedies did you find in the Bible, Nick?"

They looked at several verses together. The first thing they noticed about the verses Nick had researched was the general commands to stop worrying.

"These verses clearly tell us to put off worrying. But I think I've found what to put on in 1 Peter 5:7. It says, '*casting all your anxiety on Him, because He cares for you,*'" quoted Nick. "That means to put on prayer when we tell God about our problems, ask Him for help, and then wait patiently for His answer. In other words, I need to stop and pray about what's worrying me, not stop and eat."

"I'm looking at the surrounding verses and see that it starts with "humble yourselves" in verse 6. That's something else to put on, humility. When we humble ourselves and see how small we are, then we can call on our mighty God for help when we're struggling," added Eric. "And isn't it interesting that in 1 Peter 5:8 it is written that the devil devours. That's a graphic eating picture, isn't it?"

Nick agreed and moved on to another Scripture passage he had researched. "I was also studying Matthew 6:25-34 where Jesus is preaching to His disciples about not worrying about life issues, and Jesus includes the issues of eating and drinking. There's a parallel passage in Luke 12. I like this verse, Luke 12:25 that says, '*And which of you by worrying can add a single hour to his life's span?'*"

"That's certainly a good perspective of our humble, powerless state. Can we think of anything to put on based on that?" Eric asked Nick.

"Well, I don't see a clear command of what to put on, but I was thinking about a different take on using that verse. I could prepare a list of good activities that I can accomplish in about one hour. Things like taking a walk with my wife, doing something on her *honey-do* list, praying about the problem for one hour, or spending time with someone for my own accountability or for serving them in their need. I'm not adding an hour to my life, but hopefully, I will use that hour more productively than worrying."

"Those are great ideas to get you started. I'm going to do the same," admitted Eric. "Let me show you what I've found about our other mutual problem of eating to entertain ourselves when we think we're bored. I was thinking about this first passage in 1 Corinthians 6, but as I read through the verses surrounding it, I found more to think about." Eric read verses twelve and thirteen aloud.

"*All things are lawful for me, but not all things are profitable. All things are lawful for me, but I will not be mastered by anything. Food is for the stomach and the stomach is for food, but God will do away with both of them. Yet the body is not for immorality, but for the Lord, and the Lord is for the body.*"

Eric explained, "These verses sure give us a reasonable perspective on the main purpose of food; it is for our stomach. It's fuel. It's not for pleasing our mouths, our minds or our hearts, is it?"

"So does this mean we can only eat when we feel hungry? That seems almost legalistic, but not really realistic. By the time we feel hungry, our blood sugar level is already starting to drop off and our body is not functioning at full capacity anymore," explained Nick.

"No, Nick. Verse twelve warns us not to be legalistic. But maybe it would be a good question to ask before we eat something, 'Am I doing this for my stomach or for my mouth, or my emotions, or indulgent pleasure?' Let me tell you about what I found about tasting and enjoying our food. God not only acknowledges that we taste our food, but that He created us to enjoy sweet things, like honey. But then He uses that to teach us some other spiritual truth. Look at Proverbs 24:13-14: *"'My son, eat honey, for it is good, Yes, the honey from the comb is sweet to your taste; Know that wisdom is thus for your soul; If you find it, then there will be a future, And your hope will not be cut off.'"*

"So just as honey is good and sweet to the taste, wisdom is good and sweet to the soul," said Nick.

"Right. And how about Psalm 119:103: *'How sweet are Your words to my taste! Yes, sweeter than honey to my mouth!'*?" Eric read with enthusiasm.

"That's comparing the sweetness of honey with the sweetness of Scripture!" Nick figured. "So maybe we can apply these verses to put on wisdom and Scripture when we're tempted to entertain ourselves with food. Instead of going to the kitchen pantry, we should go to our chair and read our Bibles. I'll add that to my *to-do* list of things to put on."

"One more thing about honey," said Eric. "Proverbs 25:16 warns, *'Have you found honey? Eat only what you need, that you not have it in excess and vomit it.'*"

"That's not putting it mildly. But we need a stark warning like that sometimes, don't we?" Nick observed.

"Something else I noticed, Nick, that I think you and I should consider. I looked up the Bible references to feasts. There were plenty of them in Scripture, most of them good things. Feasts were held to celebrate weddings and honor visitors. There was even a mention of a feast for Pharaoh's birthday in Genesis 40, when he released the baker and cupbearer from the prison where Joseph waited. The most significant feasts mentioned in Scripture were those feasts dedicated to worshipping the Lord," Eric explained. "But all these feasts, given for any reason, all had something in common."

"Lots of food?" Nick asked facetiously, since he didn't see another common denominator.

"Lots of people. Nick, you and I do a lot of feasting by ourselves, don't we?"

"You're right, Pastor Eric. These verses give me another idea of what to put off and put on. I should put off snacking alone whenever possible because I'm too tempted to eat for the wrong reason. And maybe I can put on the habit of either sharing a snack with someone else, or at least checking in with someone for accountability before I eat, even just to say hi. I'm never bored with other people. I might even be so entertained by the conversation that I forget I even wanted to snack," Nick laughed at the idea.

"And that brings us back to the last two verses of 1 Corinthians 6," said Eric to focus on the final point. "Verses 19 and 20 read, '*Or do you not know that your body is a temple of the Holy Spirit who is in you, whom you have from God, and that you are not your own? For you have been bought with a price: therefore glorify God in your body.*' God wants us to glorify Him with our bodies because Jesus saved us, and the Holy Spirit dwells within us as Christians."

"Glorify God with this body," Nick repeated thoughtfully as he patted his belly.

After they had studied and discussed these Bible verses, Eric and Nick decided to finish their last topic while walking around the block of the coffee shop.

Nick and Eric agreed that their portions at the dinner table had been getting larger and larger over the years without much consideration. What little thought they had given to it included the views that they were full-grown males, the breadwinners of their home, and that they enjoyed the delicious food prepared by their loving wives who had learned what pleased their husbands.

"The fact is, Nick, my research shows that once we hit about 35, our need for more than 2,000 calories a day drops, so we should be taking smaller portions than when we were in the prime of our lives."

"Hey, I'm still in the prime of my life," laughed the jolly fellow. "No, I know what you mean, Pastor Eric. When I studied self-control, I found a few instructions to Christians to pursue self-control, such as Titus 1:7-9 and 2 Peter 1:5-7. Then I looked at the verses about the fruit of the Spirit in Galatians 5:22-24 which seems to say first that self-control is something spiritual that comes from the Holy Spirit. But verse 24 goes on to say that Christians put to death their fleshly passions. What I've discovered is that self-control is a team effort between me and the Holy Spirit. So, I need a plan of action that includes praying for help from the Holy Spirit when the going gets tough. I think this will be the verse I'll use to guard my heart, Galatians 5:22-24: '*But the fruit of the Spirit is love, joy, peace, patience, kindness, goodness, faithfulness, gentleness, self-control; against such things there is no law. Now those who belong to Christ Jesus have crucified the flesh with its passions and desires.*'"

"Good work, Nick. We've learned so much from our individual Bible studies and even more by sharing with one another the wisdom we've gleaned. I am greatly encouraged and challenged," Eric said to Nick, who looked back surprised that his pastor would respond in that way. "Let's close our time in prayer, then make plans to meet again next week. And thanks for the coffee and walk."

Chapter 20

It had been weeks since anything like this had happened. A pile of empty refrigerator bags and plastic containers lay scattered on the table next to the recliner. Remains of chocolatey desserts, crumbs from salty chips and crackers with dips, and leftover portions of previously delightful meals had disappeared. The variety of foods that had, moments ago, filled the refrigerator had suddenly disappeared without being enjoyed, barely been tasted, certainly not consumed to fuel a busy body, and been eaten without thanksgiving to God for His bountiful goodness. The television flickered and droned on and on without being closely observed, neither a comforting friend nor an effective distraction from the pursuit of the sin of gluttony. Yes, this had been an exercise in gluttony — eating way too much food for the wrong reasons. Trying to find comfort in sweets, carbs, and salty snacks had only left an uncomfortably full stomach and an achy soul.

Tears of misery and guilt eventually turned into tears of repentance. There was one ray of hope before this night was over. In the Bible, God promised to forgive any sin of anyone who would repent and believe in Jesus. Could God forgive this blatant sin of gluttony tonight? Would He? Scripture said yes.

Chapter 21

"Hey, Mom, can I tell you what I've learned about endangered animals in Africa?" Samuel asked as he cornered his mom in the kitchen.

"Sure, honey. Let me dry my hands and sit down so that I can pay attention. It looks like you have several pages of notes," Jennifer noticed as she moved around the kitchen. After she had settled on the sofa in the den, Samuel took his place standing in front of her as if he were a college professor preparing to give an intense lecture.

"First, there are a few critically endangered animals including the gorilla and rhinoceros. The mountain gorillas are caught in the middle of the civil war in Congo, plus their forests are disappearing, too. Rhinos have no natural predators, but they are hunted by humans for their horns. The endangered list includes some types of chimpanzees, zebra, elephants and giraffes. Mom, these are the classic African animals, and they are disappearing in the wild!" Samuel exclaimed with concern.

"That's true, Samuel. God commissioned people to take care of the earth and the animals. There's work to do in their native environments, and there are conservation efforts going on through zoological societies," explained Jennifer.

"I want to do more research on cheetahs. They are fast sprinters," explained Samuel.

"This is going to be an extensive project, Samuel. What does your class assignment entail?" asked his mom.

"I need to do a 10-page report plus some other creative project. Tomorrow, Dad and I are going to build an animal out of wire and covering it with papier-mâché."

"That sounds like a fun project. What animal are you going to build?" she asked.

"I want to build an African elephant. African elephants have large ears, shaped kind of like the continent of Africa. Asian elephants have smaller ears, and I read that they're easier for people to work with," Samuel explained.

"Good to know in case I ever try to tame an elephant," Jennifer teased her son.

"With all of the talk about food around church, I did some research about what animals eat, too. In the beginning, God created all animals to eat plants. Did you know that elephants are still vegetarians? They drink over fifty gallons of water and have to eat over 600 pounds of vegetation, seeds, nuts, and fruit every day. Just think about how much food Noah had to pack on the ark to feed all of those animals!" Samuel and his mom laughed together at the thought.

"I've heard that elephants are fast sprinters, too, but not as fast as cheetahs," Jennifer said to astonish her son, and he was surprised. "Elephants can run twenty-five miles per hour, but just for a short time."

"I'll check that out and add it to my report, Mom. Thanks. Do you want to know how strong elephants are?" he asked as he continued to look through his research notes. He had learned that an elephant's powerful trunk could lift over 650 pounds, and when his whole body was used to haul logs, an elephant could move over 1000 pounds. "I watched some YouTube videos of elephants pushing over trees," Samuel said.

"Maybe you could share that information about strength with Mr. Long at the exercise class on Saturday," suggested Jennifer. "He's going to be teaching us about strength training."

"That's a great idea. And we'll see grandma and grandpa there, too, won't we? I have an interesting elephant fact that they will appreciate!"

Later that afternoon, Hannah drove her mom Jennifer to the grocery store. It wasn't a long trip, but Hannah needed all the practice she could get. She carefully parked the car between two other vehicles that were lined up straight in their own spots. As they walked together towards the entrance, a disheveled woman approached them looking for a handout.

"No," replied Jennifer, looking directly into the woman's eyes with a gentle smile. "We won't give you any money today." They moved into the store.

"Mom, it's always so hard to see people like that," sighed Hannah.

"That's true, Hannah. And I hope God always keeps your conscience sensitive to be concerned for the poor and hurting. They are people created in the image of God," Jennifer reminded her daughter.

"Is there anything we can do, Mom?" asked Hannah.

"Yes, there is. But it takes a little preparation on our part. It is usually not wise or helpful to hand over cash to strangers. It's not that we're sitting in judgment, but there are many issues including safety and stewardship involved. I have an idea for a special project. Let's gather a few supplies from the grocery store, and we'll talk about it when we get home. I'm sure your brother would like to help with this project if he's not lost in the jungles of Africa working on his animal report!" she laughed.

In addition to their family's groceries, they bought brown lunch bags, bottled water, and pop-top cans of Vienna sausages. Other food items included single-serving packets of beef jerky and peanut butter crackers. Hannah was surprised when her mom selected bandages and pocket combs. At the register, Jennifer added packets of gum and mints.

"If that woman is still in the parking lot, we'll give her this," said Jennifer as she separated a refrigerated lunch meal and a bottle of water from their grocery bags.

When they got home, Eric and Samuel both came out to help unload the car. Samuel, who liked to peek in the bags for any treats from the grocery store, was surprised to see some of the extra items they had purchased for their project.

"Finish carrying in the bags, Samuel, while we unload and put things away. Then we'll work on the special project if the table is clear of animal figures," said Jennifer.

"I'll chase the safari away, Mom," joked Samuel as he cleared off their workspace.

"Please bring your markers over, Samuel," Jennifer instructed as she and Hannah carried over their purchases.

"So what's this project about?" Eric asked his wife, but Hannah answered her father.

"Dad, we saw a woman asking for a handout today in the grocery store parking lot. We didn't want to give her cash, so I asked Mom what we could do. She bought these supplies for the project," explained Hannah.

Jennifer told her family that, instead of cash, they would make bundles of nonperishable food items that they could keep in the car and distribute whenever the adults thought it was safe and appropriate. "These bundles are more than just food, though, with the bottled water that is clean and useful. The comb and bandages are helpful for hygiene and safety. And remember, Hannah, we were talking about these people being made in the image of God, and like you, they probably appreciate gum or breath mints if they're going to meet and talk with other people."

Samuel caught on. "So we can decorate the brown bags to make it seem like a present. People like to get presents, don't they?"

"That's right, Samuel. I'll also put in a Bible tract about Jesus Christ and a note about the local shelters and shower services," volunteered Eric.

In just a few minutes, the family was able to put together six bags. They put three in Jennifer's car and three in Eric's. There were some extra supplies that they would save until they needed more bags.

"Hannah, thanks for the reminder today to be prepared to serve others in need," Jennifer said to her daughter.

"We'll be ready the next time, Mom, with a bag and a happy face." With that, Jennifer was rewarded with one of her daughter's best smiles.

When the participants sauntered in the exercise class on the next Saturday, the first thing they did was set down their cans of food to be donated to the Harvest Hope Food Bank. Since many families had already taken the opportunity to go to the warehouse to serve, they were eager to support this ministry. As they looked around the recreation room, they noticed a few little props scattered at each side of the room. Although they were curious, they moved to the center where Wayne would be opening the class with prayer before giving instructions.

"This is a day that I've been looking forward to, while some of you may be a little timid about the activities today. But if you made it through the juggling lesson last month, you can do this, too. This morning we're going to work on strength training." Wayne could hear a few groans mixed in with a few squeals of interest and excitement.

"The purpose of strength training is to challenge your muscles in such a way as to make you stronger. The benefit of strength training is not only muscle development for power and shape, but also it greatly benefits the skeletal system, your bones. And while you won't be moving around at a quick pace like a cardiovascular routine, you will probably be pumping your blood, sweating and breathing heavy with this challenging workout."

Wayne continued. "Today I've brought along a lovely assistant, Pastor Eric's daughter-in-law Ashley Harvey. You all know Ashley," Wayne paused while many people greeted her and waved with a smile. "Those of you who have been around the church a while know that Ashley was a gymnast in high school, so she has a lot of experience with fitness and strength training."

"Those petite little gymnasts sure have a lot of power," said Leonard as he smiled proudly at his grandson's wife.

"We're going to divide the class today to make it easier for instructions and to carefully monitor your work with weights. We will separate the men from the women. Ashley has a special Bible verse of encouragement for the ladies while I have one for the men. Ashley, will you please recite your Bible verse?" Wayne signaled to Ashley.

"Proverbs 31:17: '*She girds herself with strength and makes her arms strong.*'"

"Oh, that's a good one for us," chimed in Beverly, while she stood next to Stephany.

"For the men, our verse is Proverbs 20:29: '*The glory of young men is their strength and the honor of old men is their gray hair.*'"

"Since I'm old, I don't have to be strong; I just have to grow some gray hair," teased Leonard as he wiped his hand on his closely shaved military crewcut.

"OK," replied Wayne with a smirk, "ladies, if you will take the north side, the guys will move over to the other side of the room. We'll meet back in the middle in about 15 minutes."

When the ladies had gathered around Ashley on their side of the room, she began her instructions. "Wayne wanted to start us off easy, and he came up with a creative way. Would each of you please go over to the collection of canned food and pick up two cans that are the same size? They are going to be our first weights!" she explained to everyone's surprise.

As Ashley began to lead the ladies through some basic arm moves, she explained that even by adding just a little weight to some familiar moves, it challenged the muscles.

"This is a great weight to start, Ashley, but what about when we're ready for more of a challenge? Should we buy dumbbells?" asked one of the energetic exercisers.

"You know that Wayne would advise that you test yourself before you invest in any equipment. You can use a variety of things as weights from around the house. If one can is too easy, grab some masking tape and put a couple of them together. Since we're donating these cans later today, I don't want to cover them in tape. You might have other objects that are easy to hold that you can use as well, like bags of beans or rice. When the time comes, dumbbells are not that expensive new, and you can probably find some at yard sales or thrift stores in pretty good condition."

"I think I have some in my garage already," commented one woman.

After going through some other moves to strengthen legs, she brought out some dumbbells of various sizes for the ladies to try. "Please remember to bend at the knees when you pick up weights," she cautioned before anyone leaned over.

In the last few minutes, Ashley asked the ladies to try to memorize and recite the verse. "Why do you think it's important for us to be strong?" she asked the group.

"We carry the kids and the groceries," said one younger mom. "We have work to do."

"My husband did the lifting around our house, but now that he's gone, I need to have enough strength to take care of myself," commented one older widow.

"I think I would look better for my husband if my arms were more shapely," observed one middle-aged woman.

"I don't think we need to worry about getting so strong that we proudly think we don't need men around anymore, like feminists," said Beverly to sum up, "but we want to be useful to serve our families, our church friends, and anyone who might need our help."

The men on the other side of the room had a challenging strength training workout with Wayne. "Come on, men," he said in his drill sergeant voice, "go for the glory of young men! And do it for the glory of God!"

After a discussion about their Bible verse, with lots of joking about gray hair, the men moved towards the center of the room. As they wrapped up their exercise class, everyone helped to load up the donated cans into boxes to be delivered to the Harvest Hope that afternoon. Over one hundred cans of food were collected that day.

"Hey Grandpa, if you let me ride over to Harvest Hope with you, I'll ride home with Dad. Then Hannah will only ask you to let her practice driving your car on the way home," Samuel said when his family was getting ready to go.

"Thanks for the warning, Samuel," replied Leonard. "Come along with us then, while it's still safe."

As they headed to the car, Samuel gave his grandparents a short synopsis of his latest African animal research. "But I learned something about elephants that I thought you might be interested in, being grandparents and all," said Samuel.

"Oh, is it about their families?" asked Beverly.

"No, it's about their wrinkles," Samuel corrected innocently. Beverly and Leonard looked at each other with smirks but tried to look seriously at Samuel for his report. "You know how elephants have so many wrinkles. Way more wrinkles than you," he assured them. "Well, their wrinkles keep them cooler because it increases their skin's surface area for air to blow on them. Plus, the wrinkles trap moisture, like the rain or when they shower themselves by spraying water with their trunks."

"Thank you for your fascinating explanation about wrinkles, Samuel. I'll try to keep that in mind. Maybe I should stop using wrinkle cream," teased Beverly.

"No wonder I'm so cool after the strength training workout. It's because of my wrinkles! I guess you need this more than I do, Samuel." And with that, Leonard blasted Samuel with a spray from his water bottle. "Is this how an elephant sprays water to cool down?" Samuel shrieked when the water hit him as he ran away.

"A wrinkle report, indeed," sighed Beverly.

Chapter 22

When Eric and Jennifer, Leonard and Beverly and the kids dropped off the donations at Harvest Hope Food Bank later that day, they took a few minutes to talk to the director in the front office of the warehouse.

"We really appreciate these donations," he said graciously. "Since you are here, Pastor Eric, would you prayerfully consider another opportunity we have coming up shortly? The local meals-on-wheels service to the homebound will be closing their kitchen for renovations next week, and we have offered to prepare the fresh meals for their delivery crew to take. That's about fifty meals for five days."

"What do you need?" asked Eric.

"We have cooked meats and vegetables covered, but what we really need are fresh baked goods: rolls, muffins, and cookies." Beverly's eyes lit up.

"Oh," she sighed. "I would love to help out with this. Since I was laid up at Christmas, I didn't get to do my traditional holiday baking, and I asked God to give me another opportunity to bake for others. With my accountability partner Stephany and several helpful ladies from church, I think we can do it!"

"It's OK with me, if there will be some leftovers," said Leonard. "But only a reasonable portion for me. Let's get your baked goodies to hungry people who need it!"

Eric had a more somber errand to run after visiting Harvest Hope. He drove over to the hospital, checked in as a visitor, and headed to the same floor where his parents had been taken after their accident. He recognized some of the staff and approached Nurse Nancy for directions.

"I'm here to see Stan Merriwether. Can you please show me to his room?" Eric asked Nancy.

"Yes, sir. He's in room 304. It's the second door on the right," she directed.

Eric tapped lightly on the door that was slightly ajar. He didn't hear noises signaling medical care nor did he hear a response to his knock, so he quietly opened the door to look in. On the bed lay the large man covered in a sheet, his complexion almost as white. Stan was connected to oxygen at his nose, and several IVs were pumping fluid and medicine into his veins. Even with machines beeping around him, Stan appeared to be asleep, as was his little wife, Betsy, who sat next to the bed, leaning her head over and gripping her husband's hand.

At the sound of movement in the room, Betsy woke up and looked over at Eric. After glancing at Stan to see that he remained asleep, she gently extricated her hand, rolled her shoulders for a stretch, and quietly got up from her chair. She motioned to Eric to follow her out of the room.

"Thank you for coming," Betsy said once they were in the hallway.

"Of course I'm here for you and Stan," assured Eric. "What happened?"

"Wednesday morning, Stan woke up out of sorts, complaining of pain in his arm and heartburn. After throwing up, he collapsed on the bed. I called 911. They came immediately and started treating him right there for a heart attack. I didn't realize they were waiting for another crew to help move Stan because he's so big. I thought of your parents who told the congregation about their accident, and how they confessed their embarrassment about being too fat to be rescued. I know just how they felt," Betsy said humbly.

She continued. "He had a triple bypass on Thursday. Those clogged arteries caused a major heart attack. I'm thankful the paramedics had arrived in time to give him some drug that prevented major muscle damage to his heart. He should make a good recovery." She dabbed her eyes at this emotional statement for a wife to make about her own husband.

"Eric, the doctor has already made comments to Stan warning about the dangers of his weight. Stan is so angry about it, but I think he realizes what a desperate situation he's in. It's good that you have come," she said again.

"Well, first and foremost, I want to bring you the love and comfort of our Lord Jesus Christ at a trying time like this. If I can encourage and exhort him at the appropriate time, I will do that too. Shall we see if Stan is awake now?" With that, Eric led Betsy back into her husband's hospital room where Stan was now sitting up after his nap, but he did not look refreshed. They prayed with him and talked for just a few minutes. Since Stan was still tired, he agreed to meet with Eric on another day. As Eric left the hospital, Eric praised the Lord for the opportunity to show love to Stan at this crucial point in his life.

Leonard thought it was best for him to stay away from home on those days when Beverly and her army of bakers were mass-producing muffins and cookies to help Harvest Hope deliver meals for the week. He found a safe haven in his daughter Jennifer's home or spent the day with Eric over at the church.

One afternoon, the two men sat down to chat after completing some minor maintenance projects around the church building. Leonard asked Eric for an update on the accountability program.

"Leonard, this has been a source of great encouragement to me as a pastor. Praise the Lord for how His people have responded to this exhortation. In a few weeks, we'll have that special celebration out at the fruit farm to honor God for the things that He has done for His people over these past months. Many great things have happened: friendships formed, peace restored, sin mortified, service increased, generosity abounding, Christians sanctified and salvation received!" Eric radiated joy over the results the Lord had accomplished in his congregation.

"More than that, Leonard, this has been a great learning experience for me personally."

"For you, Eric?" asked Leonard. "Beverly and I appreciate how you responded to our plea for help. I certainly wouldn't have said you had a weight problem before, so I just assumed that you didn't struggle with the sin of gluttony."

"I'm thankful that God in sanctifying believers patiently reveals areas of sin one at a time, rather than all at once. We would certainly be overwhelmed as young men. Even now as a mature Christian, after years of studying, meditating, applying and teaching God's Word, and by the grace of God having a conscience sensitive to God's will, looking at the sins associated with gluttony has been a new challenge. I would not have said before that I was a glutton, but after learning what gluttony is and the sins associated with it, I confess that I have sinned much in the areas of eating too much and eating for the wrong reasons."

Eric continued. "But before I drown in a sea of misery over my sin, I have found strength again in God's Word, the hope to press on. Here are the verses that I have been meditating on recently: Philippians 3:12-16, *'Not that I have already obtained it or have already become perfect, but I press on so that I may lay hold of that for which also I was laid hold of by Christ Jesus. Brethren, I do not regard myself as having laid hold of it yet; but one thing I do: forgetting what lies behind and reaching forward to what lies ahead, I press on toward the goal for the prize of the upward call of God in Christ Jesus. Let us therefore, as many as are perfect, have this attitude; and if in anything you have a different attitude, God will reveal that also to you; however, let us keep living by that same standard to which we have attained.'*

"I hope that through it all, I have not sounded like a holier-than-thou preacher looking down on my sinful congregation. I'm right in the battle with everyone on this," admitted Eric.

"No, Eric. You have tried to come alongside those of us who are struggling, and we all appreciate it. You know, every father thinks there is no one good enough for his little girl," Leonard teased his son-in-law. "You're not perfect, Eric, like that verse says. But you're real, and you're humble, and you're a loving pastor and loving husband to my little girl. Keep pressing on toward the goal for the prize of the upward call of God in Christ Jesus."

"All right. Let's heed that upward call and check on the guys repairing the roof," prodded Eric. They ended their heart-to-heart chat and got back to work.

Nick Saint opened the back door of his car to grab his lunch bag. He had been hauling this small cooler to work every afternoon for years, and it was getting pretty beat up. He would have to go to the store for a new one soon. He entered the radio station lobby, greeting the receptionist who would be there for a few more hours. Some of the salespeople were already leaving the office, heading out to meet clients or to go home after a busy work day. Most of them gave Nick a friendly greeting. If they didn't know Nick personally, people were usually nice to him because, well, he looked like Santa and they wanted to be on his good side.

Nick stopped in the booth to set his cooler off to the side, pulling out a bottle of water. Christine, the early afternoon DJ in front of the mixing board, still had some time on-air before they made the transition to his evening shift. Nick gave her a quick wave before stepping back out of the main booth. He stopped by the program manager's office to get the list of commercial announcements he needed to record before his live on-air shift began.

It didn't take long to record the announcements, so he had time to make the rounds in the offices. Usually, companies did not encourage visiting and chatting up co-workers around the office, but the radio station management wanted the DJs to make connections with the sales and promotion team members in order to foster camaraderie and enthusiasm for promotional events. The events weren't always fun, but it was an important way for the station to get out in the community to interact with their listeners. And advertisers sponsored those community events, too, which brought in more business for the station. Here in the office, Nick was a popular guy with his co-workers, and if any advertising clients were around, he was often a fascination to them.

"Hey, Nick. Good to see you!" greeted Bob in the marketing department. "Have you lost weight?"

"Yes. Yes, I have. I'm glad you noticed," replied Nick.

"Hey, we can't have Santa dwindling away in front of the kids," Bob joked. He didn't mean to be discouraging, but Nick felt as if he was being accused of hurting the kids he loved to serve.

"Well, Bill, I'm losing weight, so I will be around to see the kids next Christmas. It's not just about my health, though, but it's about my heart. I love God more than I love food, and I want to eat and drink to glorify Him." Wow, Nick had said it out loud. He had announced His allegiance to God. "I'll still be a great Santa for all the kids I see next Christmas, even if I am a little smaller."

Nick left Bob speechless, but he left the department with a friendly smile and wave. He headed back to the sound booth as Christine was preparing for her next announcement.

"Up next is Nick Saint. Enjoy the smooth sounds of *Nick at Night*." Christine wrapped up her show and switched off the microphone as the next song began to play.

After she left the booth, Nick started to arrange the booth for his five-hour shift ahead. About half an hour into his shift, he had finished his first bottle of water and went over to his cooler for more. When he opened the main compartment of his cooler, the first thing he saw was some pretty paper with a handwritten note from his wife. The note read, "I just wanted to tell you I love you and to encourage you to make food choices that would please the Lord tonight. I've made a few changes in your bag. Let me know what you think. Love you! Nadia."

Inside he found a beautifully stacked submarine sandwich. But instead of commercially packed snack bags of salty chips and rich sweets, Nadia had individually bagged healthier crackers and pretzels. He also found an assortment of fresh, crunchy crudités with a small container of ranch dip. A few sweet treats were still to be found as well.

He noticed that the portion sizes were smaller, and there weren't as many options as in the past. Nick had to admit that, in the past, he had eaten a lot of food during his evening shift, not because he was hungry, but because he was bored. Nick realized that this could be another area to examine and make changes. He said a little prayer to God, confessing his sinful eating habits. He also asked God to change his attitude during his shift not to grumble about the quiet times, but to rejoice and use that time for good. This was going to be an ongoing challenge every night of the week, but Nick was willing to work on it for the glory of God. He also wanted to remember to thank his wife for her thoughtful changes to his food bag and ask her for more help in the future.

Chapter 23

Alone again. Dinner time. Thinking about food. Seeking comfort. In the past, every lust would have been fulfilled by eating everything in the kitchen. Raid the refrigerator. Case the cabinets. Indulge in frozen treats. But there would have been no comfort; only misery, pain and the physical and spiritual consequences of overeating.

But not this time. First, cry out to God. Out loud, even when alone.

"Dear God, help me. I'm alone, and I'm tempted to run to food not to fill my stomach but to try to delight my taste senses and comfort my heart. But You say in Your Word that You will never leave me or forsake me, so I am not really alone. Your rod and Your staff, they comfort me. I need Your rod of protection and Your staff of direction tonight to do the right thing that would please You."

The prayer continued in a louder, stronger voice, "You say in Your Word that food is for the stomach and the stomach is for food, so when I'm ready to eat, it will be for the right reason. Your Word says, '*O taste and see that the Lord is good; How blessed is the man who takes refuge in Him.*' I have tasted of Your goodness and will count my blessings tonight for my delight. I take refuge in You, Lord. My heart and soul are searching for comfort and satisfaction. But I won't be satisfied with food. I will be satisfied in You and Your righteousness. I can say with the Psalmist from 17:15, '*As for me, I shall behold Your face in righteousness; I will be satisfied in Your likeness when I awake.*'"

The next decision was whether to call an accountability partner yet. With a calm heart, now was the time to try to make good food choices for dinner based on the activities of today and tonight.

There was a thick slab of lasagna left in the refrigerator, right next to some strips of veggies already cut and washed for dipping. Half of that lasagna should be plenty. Served with a nice tall glass of water to drink, a moderate slice of apple pie might be a good choice for dessert. It's fruit, after all. And homemade, too. Rather than taking the food to eat in front of the television, the table was nicely set, with soft music playing in the background. No need to get carried away with candles.

After dinner, the phone rang. The accountability partner was calling to give encouragement, but it was too late. Instead, the dear friend joined in rejoicing at the victory over the temptation of gluttony that had occurred that evening.

Chapter 24

Stan Merriwether was bundled in his robe and a blanket as he sat in his oversized, overstuffed recliner. His wife scurried around him, making sure he had everything he needed close by. She escorted Eric to a smaller chair nearby, which was obviously hers. It appeared tiny compared to her husband's monstrous chair, but it was quite comfortable. Obviously, they spent a lot of time together in their den.

"Well, I'll let you two chat," chirped Betsy as she flew away.

"Thanks for taking care of me, dear. We'll be fine for a few minutes," Stan called after his wife. Turning to Eric, he explained. "She hasn't left me alone but for a minute since I got home. She's always taken good care of me."

"She is an attentive wife," Eric complimented sincerely.

"She's feeling pretty poorly right now," said Stan.

"I'm sure she's worn out after the ordeal you have been through with your heart attack," Eric sympathized.

"No, it's more than that. She has been feeling bad ever since your sermon, Pastor Eric," said Stan. Eric braced himself for harsher comments, but none came. He waited for Stan to continue.

"You know I was hoppin' mad at you attacking me for overeating," Stan admitted excitedly, "and I'm still thinking about everything you said. I wouldn't mind talking it over with you again in a few minutes, but first I'm worried about Betsy. She's the sweetest little thing and has been the best wife to me for all these years, so I hate to see her so fretful."

"So why is she worn out and fretful, Stan?" Eric was concerned.

"I think she feels guilty for making me so fat," Stan stated flatly.

"What do you mean?" Eric asked.

"Betsy has been cooking up a storm for me these past 35 years, and I've been eating every scrap. She's a great cook, and I like everything she makes. I've been eating like the strapping construction worker I was when she met me, but I've run the business office since my dad passed it to me after we'd been married a few years. I haven't been out there doing the physical labor for a long time. But I have often come home stressed out and would eat. I felt prosperous with a nice home, good family and a table covered with food, and I'd eat it all up. Since the kids left the nest, she's still laying out the full spread, and I've still been eating it all."

Eric thought this was probably an honest description of the situation of Stan's life. Eric was attuned to some phrases that indicated some sinful eating behavior, such as eating more than what is required for actual physical activity, eating for comfort when stressed, eating out of pride to glorify self, and the long-standing bad habit of just eating too much. He wanted to gently confront Stan about his behaviors but knew they would have to address his concerns about Betsy first.

"Since your sermon," Stan began again, "Betsy has been really quiet and keeping to herself more. That may not seem unusual to you because she seems so quiet to other folks. But here in her own home, her nest, she really is a lively, chirping songbird of energy and cheer."

"I know my wife Jennifer thinks highly of her kindness and enthusiasm to serve," Eric admitted.

"I've found her crying several times, and when she finally talked to me about it, she said she was poisoning me!" Stan said.

"Poisoning you?" Eric exclaimed in surprise.

"Yes, she said she was poisoning me with too much food. She saw the situation as being her fault that I had gotten so fat. At first, I got mad at her and said I was free to eat as much as I wanted. Then I realized how serious she was, so I tried to take the blame myself. I wouldn't respond to your Biblical reproof, Pastor Eric," Stan admitted, "but I would do anything for my Betsy. But it was too little too late. I had that heart attack, and Betsy jumped to my side to take care of me like she always has."

"Stan, praise the Lord that it's not too late. You're alive. You have time to repent of your sins and to restore your relationship with your wife."

"I want to tell her again my problems are not her fault. But more than that, I want to show her that I can change. For that, I'm going to need her help."

"Stan, I appreciate how concerned you are with Betsy. I think you're right to take that burden off her shoulders, and it's noble that you want to change. But you can't do it, even with Betsy's help," Eric informed him.

"I can't change?" Stan stammered. "But I thought that's what you were preaching about!"

"Trying to fix ourselves and behave better is not what God wants us to do," began Eric. "I mean, not as our ultimate goal. That goal is too shallow, too temporal, too self-centered. No, God has bigger goals for us. He wants us to do everything - eat, drink, everything - to glorify Him."

Eric continued, "And God knows that we cannot really fix ourselves, let alone glorify Him, by our own strength. We blow it every day. No matter how good we try to be, we sin every day, so we're really not good at all."

"Hey, I'm a pretty good guy. I've been a good husband and father. I've gone to church all these years. And if I set my mind on something, I can get the job done!" exclaimed Stan in his own defense.

"Let me check what you've just said. You said that you are a good guy, but compared to who? Compared to some guy in jail for beating his wife and neglecting his children, you do seem noble. Compared to me, we might give each other a run for our money. But let's compare ourselves to God's standards. We can use the familiar Ten Commandments. Let's start with number ten which warns us not to covet. Have you ever looked at what someone else had and wanted it so much you were willing to sin to get it?"

"Yes, I suppose so," Stan admitted freely.

"As kids we see someone playing with a toy, and we grab it away. As adults, our actions may be more discreet, but the motivation is still the same," Eric explained. "Thanks for admitting that you covet, Stan. You have broken one of God's commandments. What about the other ones? The ninth commandment about not bearing false witness warns us not to lie. Have you ever told a lie, Stan?"

"Well, yeah. Everyone tells a lie now and then," admitted Stan.

"Thank you for admitting that you lie. You have broken two of God's commandments. The eighth commandment says do not steal. Have you ever stolen anything? Ever taken anything that wasn't yours without asking, no matter how small?" Eric asked Stan again.

"Well, sure, I've taken things before," admitted Stan, with less bravado.

"Thank you for admitting that you steal. You have broken another one of God's commandments. The seventh commandment states do not commit adultery. Now I'm not going to ask you to admit that you've had an affair, but the Bible says that even if we just look at another woman with lust, we have committed adultery in our hearts. Have you ever done that, Stan, in this world where men are bombarded with provocative images everywhere we turn?"

"Oh," moaned Stan, "I've broken another commandment." Stan cradled his head in his hands as Eric continued.

"There are two more commandments that address social issues, honoring our parents and murder. But so far based on your admission, you are a covetous liar and an adulterous thief. While batting .600 might be great in baseball, at 60% you're failing the goodness test. If you can't keep those social commandments, then you probably will admit that you have not been loving God with all your heart or worshipping Him only. You've probably taken God's name in vain and worshipped in an unholy manner. That summarizes the first four commandments."

"Remember the Sabbath day and keep it holy," quoted Stan. "I've been going to church regularly my whole life, but how could I have been truly worshipping God when I've broken all of His commandments without a second thought?" Stan dropped his head again and sobbed. Eric reached out to gently pat him on the shoulder. After a few minutes, Eric continued with a new tone in his voice.

"Things look pretty bad when we compare ourselves to God's righteous standards, don't they? And can you imagine standing before a judge with a rap sheet like that? Would a human judge call you good? Or would a human judge know you're guilty?"

"Guilty!" pronounced Stan.

"And no matter how you had cleaned yourself up to appear before the judge—how trim your figure, how tidy your home and family, how benevolent you appear—the judge would know that you are guilty based on the overwhelming evidence. After the verdict of guilty, now comes the punishment."

"But I've been punished enough. As good as I make things look in my life, it's been hard to live being this fat. There has been physical pain and misery. There have been cruel insults and embarrassing situations."

"Stan, those are natural consequences of sin, but that's not the punishment. You've been in church a while. What does the Bible say is the punishment or payment for sin?" Eric asked.

"*'The wages of sin is death,'*" Stan quoted Romans 6:23 flatly.

"That's right. Even for just one sin, a sinner deserves death. That's physical death and spiritual death, permanently separated from God's goodness. And remember, Stan, we don't just have one sin. You had a whole list of them." Stan shook his head. Eric continued, "But Stan. How does that verse finish?"

"*'For the wages of sin is death,'*" recited Stan carefully, "*'but the free gift of God is eternal life in Christ Jesus our Lord.'*" Stan's eyes brightened. "I've heard that verse for so long, but now I think I know what it means. I'm the sinner. I deserve the punishment, physical and spiritual death. But God is offering me a free gift of salvation. It's a gift to me, but it cost Jesus everything. He died to save me." Stan began to put together so much truth that he had been taught over the years of attending church but that he had never truly understood for himself. "I've been sitting in church, thinking I'm good enough to go to heaven, all the while breaking every one of God's commandments. Now you show me how sinful I am and that I deserve to be punished in hell forever, but then just as I'm feeling really bad about it, right away God offers to save me and give me eternal life. This is amazing!" exclaimed Stan.

"It sure is, Stan. Do you want God's gift that He is offering you, forgiveness for your sins?" asked Eric, trying to restrain his excitement.

"Yes. What do I have to do?"

"Well, there's nothing you can do to earn it or deserve it," cautioned Eric, "but when someone holds out a present to you, you have to reach out and take it. In the Bible, Jesus says in Mark 1, *'Repent and believe in the gospel.'* You admitted to a lot of sin a few minutes ago when we were working our way through the Ten Commandments. Confession is admitting sin. The more we confront our sin, the more we will understand how offensive it all is to our holy God. More than admitting we've offended Him, Christians can ask God to forgive us and to help us change."

"That sounds a lot like your accountability worksheet to mortify sin," said Stan.

"Oh, you're familiar with that?" Eric was surprised to find that Stan had looked it over. "The believing part of Jesus' instruction in Mark 1 means to learn the truth about God and Jesus, then act on that wisdom. You can't just say that Jesus was a good person and a wise teacher. He was the only truly good person, without sin. But more than that, He is the Son of God who died on the cross and rose to life three days later because He conquered sin and death before ascending into heaven where He rules as Lord and Savior. I put my trust in Jesus to save me from the punishment of my sins because He's already been punished on my behalf. I'm not trying to earn salvation, but now I'm living my life to please Him because of what He has done for me."

"And that's what your program is all about?" asked Stan.

"Well, basically, yes. If a Christian who has already been saved realizes that there is an area of sin in his life where he disobeys God, he will want to repent and obey God, mortifying the sin, because he loves Jesus so much. When I looked at my sinful eating habits in light of God's Word, I wanted to eradicate them from my life because I love Jesus so much. I want to please Him because He's already saved me. My motivation is not to earn my salvation but to please my Savior. Does that make sense?" asked Eric.

"It didn't before, but it does now. You have given me so much to think about, Pastor Eric, but I want to get this straight right now. I want that gift from God of eternal life through Jesus Christ. I repent of my sins and believe that Jesus is my Lord and Savior." Stan stated succinctly. A loud sob burst out from Betsy who was standing in the doorway. Stan held out his arms to her, and she came running.

"Betsy, honey. I'm so sorry for your pain. You haven't poisoned me. I have been poisoning myself with my sin. But that's going to change. It has changed. God has given me a gift, a greater gift that even you are to me, dear. He sent His Son to save me from the punishment for my sins. I believe, and now He's going to change me."

"Praise the Lord, Stan. Praise the Lord!" was all that Betsy could say.

Chapter 25

Finally, the day of the church picnic at the fruit farm had arrived. Since the celebration event had been postponed until July, everyone was excited to be able to pick ripe peaches in the warm Georgia sunshine. After all, peaches were everyone's favorite fruit in Georgia, and there was no summer rain in the forecast. The whole church congregation had been invited, and the planning committee had organized everything. Stan Merriwether's little wife Betsy split her time between hovering over Stan and overseeing the picnic food. Nadia Saint had enlisted her husband Nick to help her greet each arrival. They noticed that many new relationships had been forged in the accountability program, yet there were still many old relationships remaining in this united Christian fellowship. While a few people like Giselle still harbored sensitive feelings about the sin of gluttony, they had observed the changes in their friends who had participated in the accountability activities. Today, Pastor Eric planned to make a special announcement about the results of the ten-week program.

The church had been given access to a large, private picnic area for everyone to gather. Those who wanted to pick fruit could go into the designated orchards. Some people elected to pick a few ripe peaches to enjoy immediately with their picnic meal. Others wanted to pick enough for their families to enjoy throughout the week to come. Still others had big plans to bake, preserve, or freeze this ripe, juicy, flavorful fruit. The church had also organized a special gathering for some bountiful boxes to be delivered to Harvest Hope Food Bank for their hunger relief efforts in the community.

Those who had learned to juggle in Wayne Long's exercise class showed off their new talent, but only a few were brave enough to juggle fresh peaches. Most just used their beanbag balls that they had learned to juggle with. There were several family games and races with plenty of participation from the energetic group. As the afternoon wore on and people began to settle down, the worship team brought out guitars and percussion instruments to lead the congregation in songs of praise. Pastor Eric was ready to make a few comments.

"Beloved friends, it is so good to see you all here together. God's creation is beautiful, and it rejoices my heart to bask in the sunshine, play in the field, and pick the most delicious peaches I've ever tasted." Eric paused because the crowd was applauding in agreement. "We have much to be thankful for. I'm so thankful for my family: for my wife Jennifer, and her supportive parents Leonard and Beverly who continue to support and serve with us, for our younger children Samuel and Hannah, the newly-licensed driver, and for my older son Chris with his lovely wife Ashley." Eric looked around lovingly at his family.

"Hey, Dad," Chris interrupted with excitement. "While you are counting your blessings, we would like to announce a new addition to your family. Ashley is pregnant!"

"O Lord, I'm overwhelmed." Eric broke down and prayed softly. "Thank You, God, for Your goodness to me and my family. Thank You for answering our prayers for this special blessing for Chris and Ashley." Eric looked up at his congregation. "This is certainly a day for special announcements. I am thankful to see our congregation gathered together in peace and unity today. I know that we have been personally challenged to take a good look at some hard issues, but God has brought us through, and He used the fellowship and accountability to accomplish His good pleasure. I'm thankful for God's Word, the Bible, which He so graciously gave us to help us through every challenge in life. It has been a powerful two-edged sword, cutting deep into our hearts to root out sin. It has also been a soothing balm to those wounds, promising forgiveness and healing to Your beloved children. God's Word has been the means of salvation and sanctification for many this year.

"Gluttony was once a sensitive topic for many of us. God's Word on this sin has caused us to evaluate our motives for what we eat, when we eat, and how much we eat every day of our lives, three times a day. And when we applied God's Word to our lives, many of us found that we had to make changes, sometimes to little habits, and sometimes taking drastic measures.

"We have prayed. We have studied the Bible, talked about it, then studied it some more before memorizing it, decorating our refrigerators with it, and truly applying it. We have walked, juggled, and lifted weights. We have served food to others in need. And today we take time once again to joyously give thanks to God for everything He has given us.

"When we started the ten-week accountability program, we warned everyone that we would have to use some system of measurement to track progress. Those who signed up discreetly hopped on a scale and wrote down a number. A number you weren't too proud to share with anyone, but you did. When we held our last activity in April, you hopped on the scale again and wrote down a new number. Now I'm not looking for anyone to stand up and announce their new number, but if you saw a change in the right direction as a result of your efforts to apply God's Word and mortify your sinful eating habits, would you please give a little cheer right now?" Eric paused. The clapping started slow and grew louder. However, this noise didn't last long because people soon stopped clapping about their own results and started encouragingly patting the backs of friends who were rejoicing over their results.

After a few minutes, Eric continued. "I would like to give you a fantastic statistic. I don't know how many Bible verses were read. I don't know how many hours of prayer occurred. I don't know how many phone calls and texts were traded between accountability partners, but let's just say that I'm glad I have an unlimited service plan on my phone. Here is the one statistic I do know. Over 300 people registered a weight loss of at least twenty pounds over the course of our ten weeks of activities." Of course, the crowd went wild with excitement but became silent again as Eric motioned that he was ready to close in prayer.

"Thank You, God, for taking away so much of this burden. Thank You for what we have learned about You in this process, how good and generous and forgiving You are. Thank You for what we have learned about ourselves and how desperately we need Jesus Christ to save us from our sins and daily wash us from our transgressions. Thank You for sending the Holy Spirit to help us in our daily walk. May it be said of us, whether we eat or drink or whatever we do, we do it all for the glory of God! Amen."

The crowd lingered around the picnic grounds after the big announcement. Nick and Nadia Saint were talking and laughing with friends, patting others on the back and offering words of congratulations and encouragement to other victors. Samuel struggled through the crowd with a large brown bag until he reached Nick and Nadia.

"Mr. Saint? I have something for you," Samuel said politely when there was a break in the conversation.

"Well, that's very kind of you, young man," replied Nick. "What's in the bag?"

"Here, you open it." Samuel handed over the bag. Nick grabbed the handles of the bag and looked at the little crowd of friends who had gathered around. From the bag, Nick drew out...a pillow. Not a new pillow. A lumpy pillow. A pillow with a few feathers protruding from the cover.

"Well, thanks for your gift, Samuel. But why did you give me a pillow?" Nick tried to be polite after receiving the boy's unusual gift, but he wanted to understand the situation better.

"I know you have an image to keep up as a professional Santa. But since you lost weight, you don't have a belly that shakes like a bowl full of jelly anymore. So, I did some research online, and other Santas recommend lumpy feather pillows to pad their suits because they feel more like, well, like real tummy fat," Samuel said sheepishly.

Nick burst into his hearty laugh, that did, in fact, sound a lot like, "Ho, ho, ho!"

Next, Samuel moved on through the crowd to find his father. "Dad! Dad! I double-checked my calculations!" Samuel shouted as he swerved through several church members asking Pastor Eric about another ten-week accountability program.

"Hold on there, buddy. Slow down! And calm down!" Eric said as he tried to catch his son in his arms as Samuel roared towards him. Everyone around the Harveys was watching Samuel's speedy progress and wondering what the boy's excitement was about. "What calculations are you talking about?"

"Remember, Dad, when we were at Harvest Hope, I didn't do the math right. I thought we had boxed 800 meals, but really we packed 8000 meals," Samuel emphasized the difference carefully. "So I just checked my math about your special announcement, and I figured it out. I'm right this time."

"What did you figure out? What are you right about this time, buddy?" Eric asked his son, trying to match his enthusiasm while trying to figure out what the excitement was about.

"An African elephant," Samuel stated matter-of-factly as if that explained everything. Eric didn't say anything. He hoped Samuel would elaborate.

"Our church lost over 6,000 pounds, right? Three hundred people times twenty pounds totals 6,000 pounds. Well, for my safari report, I learned that an African elephant weighs about 6,000 pounds. So, our church lost an elephant!" Samuel announced. His grandparents and friends laughed at the idea of losing an elephant.

"But Dad," Samuel continued, "remember how you said that gluttony was like an elephant in the room? It was a big obvious problem that no one wanted to talk about. Because you did start talking about it, even though it was hard, and because everyone listened, even though it hurt their feelings, they started mortifying their sin of gluttony. So now the elephant in the room is gone!"

This time, when everyone around started chuckling, they could appreciate that humorous perspective on the deeper truth of the matter that Samuel was trying to make. Besides laughing for joy, they nodded their heads in agreement.

"That's right, buddy," Eric said to his young son. "Thanks for double-checking your calculations. You got that absolutely right! We lost an elephant, in more ways than one."

Chapter 26

Candlelight flickered warmly. The dark green tapers brought out the rich colors of the seasonal tablecloth and greenery of the table decorations. The mirror behind the sideboard reflected the candles' warm flames, casting a pleasant and festive glow on the dining room.

Spread across the table were many casserole dishes, deep bowls with spoon handles protruding over the edge, and serving platters stacked precariously on racks. But for a few cold dishes, everything steamed with fragrant, savory aromas of the season. Mashed potatoes and stuffing. Rolls and cornbread. Two kinds of cranberry sauce. It was tight, but in between the warm dishes were lovely ornaments and a cornucopia centerpiece in autumn hues with tangerines and nuts spilling out. Green bean casserole. Spinach salad. Fried okra and glazed carrots. The sideboard was reserved for the variety of desserts to come.

At just the right time, a gigantic platter was carried in and set at the place of honor amidst this bountiful spread. The thirty-pound Thanksgiving turkey seemed to glow as the candlelight reflected off its glossy brown skin braised with herbs and spices. Steam wafted into Eric's face as he hefted the platter into place. He looked around the room, pleased.

"Wow! What a feast!" he exclaimed to his wife Jennifer and her mother Beverly as they moved out of the kitchen into the dining room. "It looks like we have enough food for thirty people!"

Beverly and Jennifer gasped. "Didn't we get a big enough turkey?" asked Beverly with concern. "We invited over forty people to join us this year! And your parents are here, too, Eric."

Eric tried to allay their fears. "We have plenty of food to share and plenty of friends to share it with. Remember, everyone will probably be eating smaller portions this year."

As so many people gathered around the dining table as best they could for the blessing, Eric looked around the room again. He thought that everyone looked a little smaller, except Ashley who was round with his first grandchild. Beverly and Leonard stood close together, smiled, then kissed sweetly. Stephany had brought her children to enjoy her extended church family of happy, healthy people. Samuel was over by Nick and Nadia Saint who were able to join them for the Thanksgiving meal before his holiday season got too busy. Nick even wore a special bib to protect his gleaming white beard when he ate. Hannah stood by Wayne and Cindy Long, hoping to hold their active baby when they needed a break. Even Stan Merriwether and his little wife Betsy had joined them for this special evening.

When Jennifer signaled that everything was ready, Eric began to pray, "Oh Lord, we all have so much to be thankful for. Thank You for who You are and all that You have done in history and in our personal lives. First, You saved us by sending Your Son Jesus Christ to live, die, and rise again to be the propitiation for our sins. He gave us His righteousness so that we might have hope in our future reward in heaven, and we do have hope. Thank You for saving our new friend Karen at the beginning of this journey, drawing her closer to Yourself and giving her a great friend and accountability partner in Elizabeth. Thank You for saving our old friend Stan and comforting his precious wife Betsy as she continues to minister to her husband and our congregation. And thank You for Your sanctifying work in each of our lives this year. You have shown Yourself faithful and true, and Your Word has been a lamp to our feet and a light to our path. Thank You for forgiving us for our sins of gluttony. We ask for Your help, Lord, at this special feast to give us self-control in our food choices. Thank You for all of this wonderful food we can enjoy today with precious friends. May every thought, word, and deed here today be pleasing in Your sight. To God be the glory! Amen."

The End

Acknowledgments

While writing a book might be a solitary activity, publishing a book is definitely a group project. Many people deserve my thanks, and my heart feels full of gratitude toward these dear friends.

I thank God for those who teach me and point me to the Bible to address every issue of life: my pastor, John MacArthur; the original author of The Lord's Table Bible study, Mike Cleveland; the evangelistic ministry of Ray Comfort, Living Waters Ministries; and my friend Vicky Cespedes who shared her mortifying sin plan with me. I'm thankful to Dave Phillips and Liana Hofer for the opportunity to serve at Children's Hunger Fund and for the Walk At Home DVDs by Leslie Sansone that still inspire me to exercise. Thanks to Michael Hyatt for his virtual mentoring, Daniel Schwabauer for his Cover Story writing curriculum, plus everyone at NaNoWriMo.org for the virtual badges of encouragement to write a novel in November. Thanks to my family and friends who read drafts of this book: Brian McKinney, Corrie Garrett, Stephen and Judie Henry, Mae Branda, Judy Pieper, and Martha Ramirez. When Corrie encouraged me to submit my manuscript, I only dreamed of actually publishing a book, so I am very thankful to Louis Jones and his team at Dove Christian Publishing for taking me through the process.

I want to thank my husband Ross and our daughters Rachel and Anna for encouraging me, serving me, waiting for me, and keeping me grounded in real life.

Thanks be to God, the Author and Perfecter of my faith in Jesus Christ, the one true God.

Book Club Discussion Questions

I enjoy getting together with friends to talk about a good book. When my book club reads a non-fiction book, since we are all busy moms, we prefer to read one or two chapters per month before meeting to answer the discussion questions. For my fiction novel, however, I would recommend reading the entire book before trying to answer the discussion questions since you don't want to spoil any plot lines.

Even if you do not have a local group for a Book Club, feel free to share your answers on my blog post of these Discussion Questions and see the responses from other readers. In addition to these Book Club Discussion Questions, I will make available a Personal Bible Study on my website to give you an opportunity to study and consider the issues and Scripture passages used throughout this story.

1. Thanksgiving: What are some of your favorite family traditions at Thanksgiving? Do you have a special way to express thanks to God on that day? From reading this book, did you get any ideas about how to change or add to your Thanksgiving celebration? What plans can you make to set aside time to focus on Jesus during the weeks leading up to Christmas?

2. Motivation for Change: In the story, an embarrassing situation was a catalyst for change. What motivates you to make changes in your life? Have these motivations been effective to make dramatic and permanent changes to your habits and lifestyle? Do you consider pleasing God an important motivation for changing your life? Why do most people fail to keep their New Year's resolutions?

3. Sufficiency of Scripture: In Chapter 4, Leonard reminded Beverly that they have a resource of wisdom to address their weight problems: the Bible. Do you believe that the Bible is sufficient to address every issue of life (see 2 Peter 1:2-3 and 2 Timothy 3:16-17)? How has God's wisdom in the Bible helped you to deal with a difficult situation in your life? If you don't know how to find wisdom from the Bible, who can you ask for help?

4. Santa Claus: Do you think children can understand the difference between a pretend character (like Spider-Man or Santa Claus) and a real historical person (like Jesus or George Washington)? How can you teach children to discern between fact and fiction? Do you think it is important to tell children the truth?

5. Gluttony: Write out a definition of gluttony. Do you agree with the author's definition that gluttony is eating too much or eating for the wrong reason? Discuss some examples of gluttonous habits from the book or your own life. Do you agree with the author's position that gluttony is a sin? Do you understand the remedy for sin, both permanently through salvation and temporally through sanctification?

6. Elephant in the Room: Are you familiar with the old English idiom about an elephant in the room? Do you agree that gluttony is a looming issue in your home, church, or community but people try to ignore it because it is a difficult issue to talk about?

7. Mortifying sin: Mortifying sin is an old expression, but one the author likes and uses because it expresses the gravity of the issue. Write out a definition of mortifying sin. Copy the list of eight evaluation questions from Chapter 10 (or feel free to download a copy of the author's personal worksheet from the website). Would you be willing to try working through the evaluation questions the next time you are struggling with temptation or sin?

8. Food: We should enjoy food for its flavor and nutrition. What are some of your favorite foods? Why? What foods do you choose to meet nutritional goals? How can you enjoy eating food while still pleasing God? Write out 1 Corinthians 10:31.

9. Who is it? Who do you think is the character who overeats in Chapter 20? Do you think it is the same character who is tempted in Chapter 23?

10. Bad News/Good News: Do you think you're a good person? Are you good enough to deserve heaven? Review the 10 Commandments from Exodus 20:1-17. Based on God's standards, are you innocent or guilty of sin? Review Romans 6:23 to remember what you deserve. What is the gift God offers? How can you receive this gift? Have you received it? If not, do you want this gift? Pray right now to accept it!

Other ideas for a Book Club event:

- Have a potluck feast to celebrate God's goodness to create flavorful and nutritious foods. Practice self-control in portion sizes. Assign different colors for the food, or cover the five basic tastes of sweet, salty, sour, bitter and savory (umami).
- Assemble bags for the homeless like the Harvey family project in Chapter 21. After decorating a brown paper bag, fill it with food and hygiene items such as canned meat, crackers with cheese or peanut butter, granola bars, bottled water, gum or mints, a

comb, and bandages. Be sure to include a gospel tract and infor-mation about local shelter services. Serve at a local food bank or food salvage ministry.

- Deliver meals to sick friends or shut-ins.
- Start a 10-week accountability program: After everyone has read the book, get together to discuss the issues. Pair up into accountability partners. Weigh yourself and make a note. Ten weeks later, get together for a celebration. Don't forget to weigh yourself, compare the difference, and announce the results of the whole group.
- After your meeting, go out for a walk around the block.

For additional resources, visit the author's website at:
KristenHarperBooks.WordPress.com